IRON
Book
THE LAST
By A. J. Harlem

A. J. Harlem

Books by A. J. Harlem
Sin, Repent, Repeat
The Last Post
Blind Panic

**THE LAST POST: Text copyright © AJ Harlem 2020
All Rights Reserved**

With the exception of quotes used in reviews, this book may not be reproduced or used in whole or in part by any means existing without written permission from AJ Harlem.

Warning: The unauthorized reproduction or distribution of this copyrighted work is illegal. No part of this book may be scanned, uploaded or distributed via the Internet or any other means, electronic or print, without the author's written permission.

This book is a work of fiction and any resemblance to persons, living or dead is purely coincidental. The characters are productions of the author's imagination and used fictitiously.

Chapter One

Olga Umbridge spread the tiny, fragile white bones out on her bedroom windowsill. They tapped gently on the black gloss paint. Once upon a time they'd belonged to a field mouse. She'd found the little creature beside the shed, cowering next to her mum's broken terracotta flowerpots—could be useful, mustn't throw them away. It hadn't taken her long to catch the mouse, kill it, and then dissect it using the scalpel from her microscope set. She treated the latter part of the process like a biology lesson, bringing to mind Mr Kent's voice as she removed organs, setting them out neatly on a piece of white A4 paper. They were all perfect, so minuscule and delicate. Nothing like how she imagined a human's big, floppy internal organs to be.

Her phone hummed; a Facebook notification.

She frowned, hoping it wasn't the Friends For Life Group again. She'd been added to it three days ago without being asked. Goodness only knew why. It wasn't as if she even liked the Cambridge twins—Chavvy Charles and Stuck-up Spencer—or Nancy Braithwaite and Rebecca Smith-Brown. They were the cool kids, the popular ones. Trendy clothes, expensive trainers, the latest hairstyles. Hardly the category Olga fell into. Hell, had she even spoken to Charles and Spencer before?

Oh yeah, once, when they'd called her a Goth-fuck-freak. That was right. She'd stuck her finger up at them and threatened to send Satan to their door to kill their mother and bleed their father dry.

Hardly the kind of conversation that made them friends for fucking life.

With a sigh, she picked up her phone and opened Facebook.

It was a new post in the private group, this time from Nancy.

Hey, gang, I was thinking, YOLO and all that, we should go to The Moorhouse on Saturday night. Take some you know what and do you know what— wink emoji—it will be a laugh. Who's up for it?

She'd tagged all five members of the group just to be sure they all saw her invite.

Olga rolled her smooth tongue piercing on the roof of her mouth. The Moorhouse was a deserted old building a mile and a half from the road between the villages of Brayton and Northbury. Part of it had been destroyed by fire years ago, and since then it had sat abandoned, the roof and walls slowly sliding downwards and nature taking over, crawling into the window frames and twining over the pockmarked brickwork. Olga loved the old ruin and often walked there on her own, listening to Sisters of Mercy or Siouxsie and the Banshees as she tramped over the fields. There was something comforting about the place. The way it didn't apologise for the way it looked, for its disrepair and broken aloneness.

Her phone came to life again. A message from Charles, replying to the post.

Hell yeah, try and stop me. Just what we need.

Then his twin, Spencer, older by one minute, or so she'd heard, popped up.

Only if we all go. All five of us in this group. That means you, too, Olga.

Olga frowned and scratched her chin. Why was Spencer so keen for her to go? It must be a joke, surely. Tall, blond, handsome enough to be a model, Spencer was hardly her type—or rather it was the other way around, she, Olga, wasn't his type. His last girlfriend, Celeste Trent, had been from South Africa. A leggy blonde with baby-blue eyes, a caramel tan, and never without her Tiffany necklace, earrings, and bracelet. She'd moved back to Cape Town three months ago.

Finally got Celeste out of your heart—heart emoji—and made room for a new love.

That post was from Rebecca and was accompanied with a GIF showing a chubby cupid firing an arrow.

"What in the Devil's name." Olga wrinkled her nose. If she were the type of teenager to harbour fantasies about one of the coolest twins to have ever lived fancying her, that was exactly what she'd think. But Olga was a realist. With her long witchy skirts, graveyard complexion, and eye makeup so dark the neighbours gave her wary glances, Olga new better.

Olga, I know you're there. Say you'll come with us.

That was Nancy again.

Olga stared outside, confusion a spiderweb spinning around her mind. She didn't focus on the little birdbath in the middle of the back garden, currently stringed up with red balloons—her mum liked red balloons this week, last week it had been green—because her thoughts were colliding. Most of the time she didn't care that she was a loner. That she didn't have a best friend to confide in or anyone to hang out with at college. But right now, someone to bounce this perplexing situation off would be just the ticket.

A new notification popped up. A private message.

Spencer.

He'd contacted her directly.

Her mouth dried. Her heart rate picked up. Perhaps it was true. Maybe he did like her.

"Shut up, you stupid bitch," she muttered. "Of course he doesn't." She placed the phone down, next to the bird bones, and stalked to the opposite side of her bedroom. Once there, she flattened her palms on a glossy poster of The Cure and took long, deep breaths. "Ignore him. Ignore him. Ignore him."

But she couldn't. The desire to see the content of the message was like an itch she had to scratch.

Mumbling, she stomped back to the windowsill and scooped up her phone. She opened the private message, a swirl of nausea spinning in her guts.

Olga, I really want you to join us. Please say you'll come. Spencer x

She shook her head. What the fuck was going on? And now she'd have to reply because he'd know she'd read the message. "Jesus H Christ, I don't have to reply." Again she put the phone down.

She walked to her dressing table, grabbed a brush, and began to drag it through her hair. She'd washed it earlier, and it was smooth and glossy, black as raven feathers with the tips the colour of rain-wet moss.

She peered into the mirror. She wasn't wearing her usual dark lipstick, not today, and her lips were the only nod to pink she could ever tolerate. "Spencer Cambridge does not fancy you. This is a joke."

Yes, that was what it was, a joke. In fact, that was what she'd reply with.

She slammed down the brush and marched to the phone, not caring, for once, that the banging might upset her mother. She swiped it up.

Stop fucking me around, wanker! Why would you want me there? I'm hardly in the 'it-club'

A reply came back in seconds.

Whoa, sorry, Olga, I'm just being friendly. That's why we want you there. You never have anyone to hang out with. It's Saturday night. Middle of summer. Best years of our lives and all that—sun emoji, sunglasses emoji.

Olga stared at that. So the fuckwit felt sorry for her. Pity wasn't something she needed. Pity could go swivel. She'd had enough do-gooders over the years throwing that shit around.

I don't need friends. Go screw yourself. Your brother, too!

Twin fetish, huh. I suppose we'd consider it—smile emoji—if it's a fantasy of yours.

Olga's mouth hung open. What the hell...? She hovered her finger over the letters again. How should she respond to that?

A sudden image popped into her head. It was uninvited, unwanted, and full of its own damn self-importance.

Spencer and Charles Cambridge, naked, their attention on her. All six-pack, suntan and muscle, and very lickable.

Her heart pounded. That was not a fantasy. No way. She'd never even thought of them naked before. Or maybe...

She swallowed.

There had been that one time. At the college swimming gala last year. When they'd been in the finals for the breaststroke. She'd had a great spectator seat, right by the start line. Watching them warm up, swinging their arms, puffing up their chests hadn't been a hardship.

A warm tingle travelled up her spine, the memory heating her.

Olga?

What?

Come out with us, to The Moorhouse. It will be fun. I want to get to know you better – smile emoji

I'm leaving this stupid Facebook group. Goodbye!

Don't leave it. Please!!!

She frowned. *Why not?*

I don't want you to

Why do you suddenly give one fucking hoot about me?

I always have, it's just... Celeste was around. You know. And now she's gone, we're not together anymore, I thought perhaps we could...sorry, I'm being stupid.

She was the one being stupid. To even be engaging in a conversation with Spencer Cambridge. Blokes like him didn't chat to Goths like her. Didn't want to be friends with oddballs. It wasn't the way the world worked. Another message popped up.

I just thought that there was something between us, Olga. A spark. That there could be more. The spark could become a flame. I know we wouldn't be a conventional couple, and it would shock the heck out of some people, but so what. Me and you. I think we're worth a go.

Olga rubbed her temples and reread his words three times. Me and you. Worth a go.

Last I checked, it wasn't April Fool's Day, Spencer. So stop fucking me about. I'm going now!

Please, Olga, don't go. Meet me. We'll walk to The Moorhouse together. Talk. Properly.

About what?

About why Nancy added you to the group

Tell me now

It's embarrassing

So. Say it. Or I won't meet you. Had she really just written that? Now if he did say it, she'd have to meet him. Stupid cow, that was what she was. The last thing she wanted to do was meet up with Spencer on Saturday night and go for a walk in the sunset with him...wasn't it?

Okay, I'll tell you. I've liked you for a long time, Olga. Charles, Nancy, and Rebecca know that. And I've been struggling to pluck up the courage to ask you out.

"Ha, ask me out," Olga blurted then laughed. "As if." She swirled her finger over the mouse bones, spreading them out, then pushing them back together again into a little pile of death.

I know you don't believe me, but it's true. Don't reject me now I've stuck my neck on the line, please. Meet me. Let's talk it through...I know I can make you see how I feel about you.

"How he feels about me." Olga hated to admit it, but a tiny kernel of hope was growing. Spencer was saying the words she'd longed to hear from a boy. But never in her wildest dreams had she ever thought it would be from him.

He sent another message. *I'll be there, waiting. At the five-bar gate, the one that leads from the lane to The Moorhouse. We'll walk together. Say yes... x*

"Fuck, fuck, fuckity fuck." She tapped her tongue stud on her teeth. Now what the devil was she going to do? If she didn't go, she'd always wonder what-if. And if she did, she'd be setting herself up for heartache. He didn't really like her. He couldn't. That wasn't the kind of person she was...likeable. If she was, she'd have friends. People wouldn't call her freak, weirdo, Satan's child.

Okay. Seven o'clock. Bring cider. Had she really just agreed to this?

Fantastic. Yes. See you then, beautiful. Can't wait. X

Beautiful! She turned her phone upside down, placed her elbows on the windowsill, and rested her face in her hands. She was used to bizarre and fucked up, it was the way her life was, but this, this was a whole new level of crazy.

Chapter Two

"Hi, Shona," Meredith, Shona's hypnotist slash therapist said. "How has your first week on the new job been?"

"Always a good week when you put a murderer behind bars."

"Oh yes, I saw that on the news. Talk about getting a baptism of fire, eh."

Shona sat on the couch set in the recess of the bay window. She pulled in deep breath. Meredith's home office had a much-needed air of calm to it. The gentle ticking of a mantel clock, the spread of green from the garden, and the polished wood-panelled walls made everything else fade into the distance. "And everyone keeps trying to convince me Ironash is such a quiet place. That nothing ever happens here."

"We know that's not true." Meredith gathered a notebook and pen from her wide mahogany desk, then took a seat near Shona. She crossed her legs, her pale-blue skirt falling in soft folds.

"Unfortunately you're right." Shona thought of the sketch she had in her office desk at work. The face of her attacker. His image drawn from her memory—a memory Meredith had helped her dig out. It was the first rung on a very long ladder to justice.

"So what are you hoping to get out of today's session?" Meredith asked.

"More evidence, well, you know, not concrete, obviously, but something for me to go on."

"The memories from last time were helpful."

"Yes. Very. I need more like that."

She raised her eyebrows. "And you feel ready for them?"

"As ready as I'll ever be." Shona huffed. "When is there a good time to remember an assault?"

"I suppose never." Meredith smiled gently and tipped her head. "Sit back, relax. For a few minutes I want you to let your breathing calm, your eyelids grow heavy, and concentrate on the ticking of the clock."

Shona toed off her shoes and swung her legs around on the couch. She settled into the soft cushions, her head resting back and her hands clasped on her stomach.

"See if you can release the tension in your fingers," Meredith said.

Shona moved them to her thighs, palms flat on her white jeans. She blew out a breath through pursed lips.

Tick. Tick. Tick. Tick.

After a few minutes, Meredith spoke again.

"Focus on your breathing. In and out. In and out. Sense the air on the tip of your nose, the inside of your nose. Your throat. Your chest, the top and the base, feel it in your belly." She paused. "Your conscious thoughts are slipping away, nothing else is important but your breaths and being here, with your memories."

Shona felt herself closing inwards, being drawn towards a dark place that contained only her, the very bones of her soul.

"And now visualise the staircase you're going to walk down. It's right before you. There's a handrail, you're safe. You're strong, you're safe. Take the first step."

In her mind, Shona did just that.

"And the next and the next. I'll let you count them yourself, take your time. With each step feel yourself connecting more and more with the past, delving deeper into the recesses of your mind."

Meredith was quiet for several minutes. Shona, having done this exercise before, went down the stone steps and into a room, that unlike her mind, wasn't dark. It was bright with a dense white fog.

"Now you're there." Meredith's voice sounded distant, almost underwater. "I want you to remind yourself that no harm is about to come to you. You are in control here. You are safe."

"I am in control," she whispered. "No harm will come to me."

"And with that knowledge, walk around. Use your third eye, your intuition, to feel your way, find what you need to find."

Shona let her thoughts dissipate completely. All she needed was this room. It held the keys to unlocking the rest of her life, and Tina's.

A face loomed before her. One she'd seen before. Dark-skinned, thick monobrow, gappy front teeth. It was more detailed this time. The brown of his eyes reminded her of shiny conkers, and a string of spittle sat in the corners of his lips.

Her instinct was to recoil, but she stayed with it, despite the fact she hated him. Hated the way he looked, the way he smelled—strong, spiced aftershave.

"It's okay, stay with it," Meredith said. "What else is there?"

"I can't..." She swallowed, the familiar rise of nausea gripping her stomach.

"You're strong. You're safe. You need to look around, Shona."

Shona steeled herself, fought the urge to turn and run back up the steps. She was here for a reason. She wouldn't leave without getting what she wanted.

She turned her attention from the face and was greeted with the bright light again. It was white-hot, brilliant, dazzling. But as she stared, something took shape. It was a small grey statue. It had a face, tightly coiled blobs of hair, half closed, meditative eyes, and held one hand palm up, the other resting on its crossed knees. "I see...I see a..."

"What? What do you see?"

"It's a statue, grey, I think it's of Buddha."

"Good. Okay. What else is with the Buddha?"

"Nothing, just fog...I..."

"Keep going. You're doing so well, Shona. You're safe to stay there."

The Buddha was in sharp focus now, she could see it clearly. Small gold marigold flowers sat beside it, their little heads plucked off and scattered.

"Keep looking. What you need is there. Don't judge, don't analyse, just see."

Shona stared at the fog hiding her memories. The more she concentrated, the more the cloud seemed to be evaporating, thinning.

Her heart rate sped up, but she willed it to stay calm.

I am safe.

A melody of colours was looming before her. Set in a strange, geometric pattern, blue, orange, red, yellow, and green grew from dull to bursting with brightness. "There's a circle, surrounded by a square...it's..."

"Describe it, Shona. You can do it."

"It's intricate, big, it's every colour."

"A picture?"

"No, it's seems softer. Fabric...maybe a rug." But that didn't seem right. If it was a rug it was up in the air, before her. She could see it ahead while standing.

Suddenly, from in front of the pattern, a person appeared. A man. Not the dark-haired one from before. This bloke had pale hair, not quite blond. He was facing away from her. His ears stuck out.

Shona tensed.

He faded.

"Relax, Shona. Stay there, you're doing so well. Get all the information you can."

She forced her concentration back. She had to do this. See it through...see him.

He turned; it was like slow motion. First she saw his protruding pink ears, then his profile—weak chin, hooked nose, thin lips—and then his full face.

Again a shiver of disgust wended down her spine. She knew, without doubt, she was seeing one of the men who'd taken her and her friends. This creep was a rapist.

And now she'd seen him.

"This bitch, Tina, she's mine," he said. "Stay the fuck away from her, Vince."

"Vince," Shona whispered. "Vince."

He leered closer, eyes so wide she could see the whites.

Her chest tightened. Breathing became difficult. She backed away, escaping him. His hands came up, fingers spread, and between them a length of rope.

"Fuck, no…" She gasped, clutching her chest.

"It's okay, Shona, you're safe. Turn around and come up the staircase. I'm with you, each step. You're safe."

She kept her eyes closed. Visualised the steps in place of the man, then mentally ascended, counting each one.

By the time she reached the top, her breaths were easy to catch again and her heart not thumping quite as wildly.

"Before you open your eyes, describe what you saw, while it's still fresh."

"Yes. Okay." She relayed the man's features, and again what she could remember of the pattern which seemed to have burned into her memory. What on earth was it? It seemed so organised, so symmetrical. Was it a sign? A logo?

"Vince," Meredith repeated. "Is that this man's name?"

"No, he was speaking to Vince. Someone called Vince." She opened her eyes, blinking in the harsh light of the day. "He was telling Vince to stay away from Tina." She paused, her friend's name on her lips filling her with sadness for what Tina's life had become since that night. "He wanted her, this bastard, this fucking creep, he wanted her for himself."

A familiar sense of black rage swelled in Shona's chest. It was one that could overtake her thoughts if she let it. So she battled it down, kept her train of focus. At this point in her life, more than ever, she had to allow sense, facts, and evidence rule. Not her emotions.

Easier said than done.

Meredith stood. She went to a jug of iced water with cucumber slices bobbing in it and poured some into a tumbler.

"Here, sip this." She gave it to Shona.

Shona was glad of the refreshing taste. It got rid of the memories of revolting scents and flavours. It was strange, though, how the men's aftershaves seemed to coat her tongue, her throat, as well as fill her nose. It wasn't a cologne she recognised.

Meredith took the glass and passed Shona a pad of paper and a leather case of coloured pencils. "Draw this pattern you described. Right now, while it's still vivid."

"Good idea." Shona took a red pencil. She sketched a circle. Within it she drew a square with gaps in the sides, four of them, like entrances into a maze. Then at the centre a circle. She filled it in with yellow and orange, blue and green. It was a vibrant image, detailed, too, but still she couldn't decipher it.

"Do you know what it is?" She held the finished image up towards Meredith.

She studied it, a frown creasing her brow. "No, not at first glance." She rubbed her chin. "Something vaguely familiar about it, though. Perhaps it will come to me."

Shona swung her legs around and slipped her feet into her sandals. "If anything comes to you, drop me a message."

"I will."

"Do you want this copy?" Shona asked.

"No, you keep that, but perhaps I'll scan it, so I can revisit it."

Shona handed it over. What was that pattern? What did it mean? Was it a clue to where they'd been taken after they'd been drugged? Was it a clue to the identity of the men? Or was it just some random pattern, something her mind had come up with in her moment of absolute horror, so she had a focal point, something to concentrate on while he was…?

She stood, placed her hands on her hips, and paced to the window.

Meredith's garden was so beautiful. Manicured to within an inch of its life, it was a haven of peace and tranquillity. Several sparrows played in a stone birdbath.

For a moment Shona found herself wishing she was one of them. Sparrows didn't worry about solving date rape cases, proving their worth in male-dominated roles, or living and breathing every moment with the need for vengeance.

"Here, study it often." Meredith returned the image to Shona. "What it means will likely come to you at the most unexpected moment."

"I will, thanks."

"And show it around at work, to your partner—"

"Oh no. I can't do that."

"You can't?" Meredith raised her eyebrows.

"No."

"Why, isn't your new partner what you hoped? I know you were apprehensive about working so closely with someone you didn't know at all."

"No, it's not that. He, Earle, is really nice. Or at least he has been so far. Smart, professional, knows when to speak and when to shut up." She smiled, though there was tension in her face. "I like him. I think we'll be a good team going forward."

"But you can't show him this?"

"I haven't told him about the incident eight years ago."

"Are you going to?"

"I'm not planning on it."

Meredith's silence stretched on. Her eye contact didn't waver from Shona's.

"You think I should?" Shona asked eventually.

"If he's smart, won't he figure out there's something else going on with you? Another reason for your return to Ironash? You gave up a good career path with the Met."

"I want to do this on my own. Find these lowlifes and nail them. This isn't Earle's problem."

"Would he see it that way?" She paused. "Don't coppers view all criminals as their business?"

"I applied for the transfer stating family reasons, not that my new boss, Fletcher, seems to remember that from the forms." She turned to face Meredith. "So if Earle or anyone else finds out it's because I have scores to settle, it will make me appear unprofessional." Shona had spoken harsher than she'd intended to. "There's no way I'll let anyone call me unprofessional after all the years of hard work it took to become a DI."

"Okay." Meredith nodded. "If that's the way you feel."

"It is." Shona tipped her chin. "Same time next week?"

"Absolutely." Meredith smiled. "See you then."

Chapter Three

Olga dragged the thick black liner beneath her eyelids for the fourth time. She was really going for density today. And why the hell not? If Spencer liked her Goth style, she'd give it to him full-on. See if he really was telling the truth about fancying her.

Fancying me? Yeah, right.

She applied matt black lipstick. When she'd first started wearing it a few years ago, she'd shocked herself when she'd looked in the mirror. Against her powdered skin it was startling.

Deciding it was a special occasion, Olga took the lid from her one bottle of perfume, Poison. Her mother had bought it during a manic shopping spree three months ago. Many things had been returned to the shops or the catalogue when the credit card bill came in and the mania receded to abject depression, but the perfume had been opened, used, it couldn't be returned.

She sprayed it on her black velvet blouse, the metallic, plummy scent infusing into the material. The blouse, one of her favourites, had a small rip in the seam, at her left side, but she didn't think anyone would notice. Besides, teamed with her short leather skirt, it worked.

After adding leather fingerless gloves and biker boots, she headed out of her bedroom. It was time to break the news to her mother that she was going out for the evening.

"Mum, want a cup of tea?" she called as she walked past the door to the living room.

"No."

"Okay, I'll make it now." Her mother always said no, but Olga made her one anyway. She needed to drink more. She'd had a kidney stone two years ago.

After she'd made the tea, she took it into the living room. Her mother sat on the sofa in a pink velour trackie. She was surrounded by red balloons—they spread like a carpet over the floor, were attached by string to the ceiling light and balanced on the bookshelf, jostling for position.

"Here you go, two sugars." Olga set the tea down.

"Thanks, pet." Her mother didn't look up from the metallic scratch picture she was frantically scraping at.

"I'm going out for a while, Mum."

"Okay."

Olga raised her eyebrows. Not what she'd been expecting. Maybe the good-luck demon was on her side. "I'll be back later. I'll make you another cuppa."

"Okay."

"I've got my phone if you need me." Olga walked to the living room door. Perhaps her mother was coming out of the mania? Which meant depression would hit soon, but often there were a few weeks of almost normal behaviour between the two extremes. Olga savoured them when they happened.

"Wait! Wait! Olga, you're going out? Where? No. Something might happen to you?"

Olga sighed, rested her fingers on the handle of the door, and turned. "I'll be fine. I'm meeting some friends."

"What friends? You don't have friends. You told me that. You don't have friends, Olga."

Olga bit back the pain that statement induced. But perhaps it wasn't quite so true now. Four people from college, cool people, had invited her out on a Saturday night. Maybe they were all growing up, and being different didn't mean she couldn't socialise...have a boyfriend. "I've made some friends, Mum."

"Where? Where have you made them? On the Internet? That's bad. You can't go."

"At college. I met them at college."

Her mother wrung her hands and bit on her bottom lip.

"It's okay, really, Mum. I'll be back later."

"You said everyone at college was hateful, that you wished they'd all go to Hell and burn for all eternity."

"I know, but these ones…well, I think they might be different. They've been nice to me."

"They have?"

"Yes, so you know…maybe it's time I stopped being such a loner."

"You said you liked that. You like being on your own."

"And I do, but…"

"But you don't want to end up a weirdo like me." She stabbed at her chest with her thumb. "A woman whose husband upped and went because he couldn't cope with balloons."

Olga knew full well it had been more than the balloons that had made her father leave. It had been the hysteria, the plate-smashing, the drink, the dinner invites to complete strangers. Taking in any animal that needed a home. Police visits, social service visits, the endless busybodies. No wonder he'd got on a plane to Australia ten years ago and hadn't been heard of since.

Spineless git. He could burn in Hell, too. What kind of man left his daughter to cope with this shit?

"So I'll be back later," Olga said. "Maybe you should go into the garden, get some fresh air before the sun sets."

"No, the balloons need watching."

"There's some in the garden still, you know."

"There are?" She jumped up. "I should get them, they might pop." She shuddered. "Can't have that, poor things."

Olga curled her fingers around her small purple handmade bag as her mother rushed past to collect her precious balloons. She'd make her escape now. If any of the balloons had burst, it would be an hour of mayhem and upset.

She slipped out of the front door, pulled on her shades, and headed for the west side of the village. Usually she'd listen to music, but today she was happy to be lost in her thoughts.

Last night she'd dreamed of Spencer. It wasn't what she'd expected, but even so, it wasn't unpleasant. He was tall, handsome, and smiley. They'd gone to the zoo—one of Olga's best places—and hung out in the reptile house. There'd been dark corners, it was hot, sweaty, there was no one else there. And right before she'd woken up, he'd kissed her.

She'd greeted the day with her heart racing, a tingle travelling over her skin, and a sense of excitement fluttering in her belly.

But as she walked towards the lane and the five-bar gate they were meeting at, she began to doubt herself again.

What if this is a cruel joke?

Does he really want there to be something between us?

As she got closer, she decided that if he was there at all it would be a bloody miracle. They'd probably be sitting down the park, laughing at the fact they'd sent the college freak on a wild goose chase.

She stroked her tongue around her teeth, the small silver ball comforting against the enamel. The sun was setting, the warmth bleeding from the day—but it wouldn't get deathly cold, not in August. Likely the bats would be out soon, too, collecting the midges from over the cornfields. She liked watching the bats.

It was then she saw him.

Pacing beside the gate, he had his hands shoved into his jeans pockets and head bowed. The sun glinted off the blond strands of his hair as though weaving them with gold.

Her heart did a weird somersault. Her belly clenched. Spencer Cambridge, *the* Spencer Cambridge, was waiting for her. And by the looks of it he was alone, the others in the Friends Forever Group nowhere to be seen.

For a moment her steps faltered, nerves washing over her. What would she say? What would they talk about? Should she really have gone so overboard with the thick makeup and black lipstick?

Yes, it's who I am.

She tipped her chin, set back her shoulders, and strode ahead, her boots clomping on the lane.

He stopped, glanced up, saw her, and waved.

She found her hand rising, waving back. What the fuck?

She dropped it to her side, frowned, and paced faster.

"Hi," he said with a smile when she reached him. "I was worried you'd be a no-show."

"It's a nice evening for a walk. It was no odds to me whether or not you were here, Spencer." She stopped and put her hands on her hips.

He chuckled, a lovely deep sound. "Well I'm glad you're here." His attention dipped from her face, over her blouse—unbuttoned to her cleavage—her leather skirt, long legs encased in ripped fishnets and chunky boots. "And you are gorgeous."

"Yeah, right."

"You are." He held out his palms. "What can I say, I like the Devil worship look."

"I don't worship the Devil." She frowned.

He laughed again and pointed at her. "And that is why I need to get to know you better. So I don't presume stupid stuff like that."

"Devil worship isn't necessarily stupid, it just isn't my thing."

"So what is your thing?"

She shrugged. "I'm an atheist, though I lean towards paganism."

"Ah, I see."

"You do?"

"No, not really, but you can explain on the way to The Moorhouse. Come on, this way." He opened the gate just enough for them to slip through. "There's no bulls in here, or at least I hope not."

"No, there won't be. This is a wheat field." She gestured to the swaying crop. "It will be harvested soon, in the next week or so."

"You know about farming?" he asked, closing the gate.

"Not really. I just walk a lot around here."

"On your own?"

"Of course." She set off along the hard, packed-earth path that cut across the middle of the field.

He fell into step beside her, his fancy trainers silent. "You used to hang out with Stacey what's-her-name, didn't you."

She glanced at him. He wore a red polo shirt, and pale freckles were sprinkled over the bridge of his nose. "How do you know that?"

"I've been watching you, from afar." He winked. "But you guessed that, right?"

"No, I bloody didn't." She shrugged. "And Stacey moved to Scotland, with her father's job, you know."

"Ah, I see."

She caught a whiff of his aftershave. It was sweet, fruity, something expensive and trendy, no doubt. She wondered what he thought of her Poison.

"You really didn't notice?"

"Notice what?" She stared straight ahead, at the copse which signalled the halfway point to The Moorhouse.

"Me watching you?"

"No." She shrugged.

"Not even in biology?"

"You sat behind me last year, how could I?"

He laughed. "I suppose you're right. I just thought you'd feel my eyes on you."

"I'm not psychic, you know."

"So what are you? If you don't mind me asking."

She stopped and faced him.

"But if you mind me asking." He held out his palms. "I won't."

"What do you mean? What am I?"

"Well...this...the black, the t-shirts with weird bands no one else has heard of."

"Of course other people have heard of the music I listen to. Just because you and your cronies haven't, doesn't mean it isn't popular in certain circles."

"Cults, you mean?"

"Cult? You think I'm in a cult?"

"I don't know."

"For fuck's sake." She stalked off, continuing in the direction they were going in.

"Olga." His fingertips brushed the top of her arm. "Forgive me, I'm an idiot. It's just..."

"What?"

"I see you from afar. Beautiful but never with a smile, and you intrigue me. I want to stop guessing and know the truth."

"The truth?"

"Yeah, what's going on?" His voice was soft, gentle...enticing. "With you?"

"Nothing."

"There is something. I can sense it. I think maybe I'm the only one that can, Olga. Talk to me."

Her throat tightened. It was the nicest anyone had spoken to her in a long time. It cut through the tight protective bands of steel she had wrapped around her heart. They kept out pain, humiliation, and desolation. But Spencer...he'd just unlocked the bolts.

"Tell me about home," he said.

"Home." She pulled in a breath. "Can be like a party or a war zone, depending on Mum's mental health."

"Shit, really."

"Yeah, really."

"But your dad helps out, right?"

"What dad?" She swiped at a head of wheat, decapitated it, then set about pulling off the seeds and discarding them.

"He's not around, eh?"

"Is yours?" she asked.

"Yes."

"Then you're lucky. You and Charles. To have a dad." She wanted to add 'rich' to that sentence but stopped herself. Money wasn't what this conversation was about.

"Yes, we are lucky." He paused. "Being a twin isn't always the best fun, though."

"Why not? Seems to me you guys run the show at college. Charles and Spencer Cambridge call the shots, set the trends, make or break a party."

He burst out laughing. "Is that really what you see?"

"Yeah."

"Well, it's not like that." Again he touched her arm, lingered this time.

"So tell me what it's like." A quiver of sensation went up to her shoulders, her neck, and over her scalp.

"Yes, we have friends, never miss out on a party invite, but it's not all a bed of roses."

"I don't believe you have any thorns in your bed to contend with."

"Being popular," he said, reaching for her shoulder and drawing her to a halt, "isn't all it's cracked up to be."

She looked up at him. The sun was behind him, creating a halo around his head and neck. He really was the most handsome bloke she'd ever seen.

"It's hard," he went on, resting both of his hands on her shoulders now. "To always be watched, second-guessed, emulated."

"Yeah, really tough."

"It is." He smiled, just a small tilt of his lips. "I envy you."

"Why the hell would you envy me?"

"You're your own person. You're confident in your skin, wear whatever the fuck you want to, listen to music you like, not because it's popular. I want to be like you. Be true to myself." He tipped forward.

His breath was laced with mint. She could almost count the freckles over his nose.

"So just do it," she said in a whisper. "Just be yourself. Do what you want."

"Do you mean that?"

"Yes."

"Including this."

Suddenly his lips were on hers, his tongue stroking into her mouth, touching against her piercing.

Her eyes were wide open.

His were closed.

Shock had her knees weakening and her spine turning to dust. But still she kissed him back. She didn't know if she was doing it right. It was her first ever kiss.

And then he pulled away. His lips were blackened from her lipstick. His eyes sparkled.

"What did you do that for?" she asked, her voice a little shaky.

"You told me to do what I wanted. I wanted to kiss you." He tucked a strand of her hair behind her ear.

"Why?"

"Because I've been thinking about doing that for a long time."

"Oh." She wiped her lips then pointed at his. "You have...black..."

"Have I?" He rubbed his mouth then grinned. "We should get going. The others will be waiting, and the cider will be getting warm."

Suddenly a cider was exactly what she wanted—something to settle her racing heart and her firework hormones.

Spencer Cambridge just kissed me.

If she'd had a best friend, Olga would have been sending a secret text to fill her in on the hot details.

But of course, she didn't have a best friend. Not since Stacey had left then stopped answering messages. Out of sight, out of mind.

Yet. Maybe Rebecca and Nancy would be her new friends, the way she'd told her mum they were.

Chapter Four

"Hey, Olga, you did come." Nancy waved from where she sat on a red-and-blue picnic blanket. She had a wide smile on her face as her attention flicked between Olga and Spencer.

Just past the copse, Spencer had reached for Olga's hand and entwined their fingers. She'd been shocked at first, thought about pulling away, but then realised she liked his big warm palm against hers and the heat radiating from his blood and skin, into her blood and skin.

So she'd walked with him that way, chatting about their shared lessons and her love of TV shows *Dexter* and *Making a Murderer*—he hadn't seen any of them. At first, she'd felt uncomfortable talking so freely, but walking and having a conversation was better than having to sit and stare at someone while she spoke. She didn't like that. People always studied her as though she were an oddity.

Spencer, however, was treating her differentness as though it intrigued him in a good way. Not the usual bad way.

If only the nervous fluttering in her belly would go. It was like she'd swallowed a damn spider and it was running around in there.

"Here, have a cider, they're still cold." Rebecca handed her a can of Strongbow from a blue cool bag.

"Er, thanks." It was the first time Rebecca had ever spoken directly to Olga. Oh, she'd heard her voice before, of course she had, it was all singsong and light and terribly, terribly posh.

"You've got some catching up to do," Charles said, raising his can. "We're on our third."

He was sitting at the top of a set of stone, ivy-edged steps that led into The Moorhouse. Like his brother, he wore faded Levi's and a polo shirt, though his was blue. It had the same logo on the right side of the chest. Olga wasn't sure what the brand was, but it was bound to be a high-end designer.

"Here, pass me one," Spencer said.

Olga released his hand and popped the ring pull. She took a long slug, letting the cool, sweet liquid coat her dry throat. Each swallow assured her the alcohol buzz was on its way. And boy did she need it. This was a surreal situation.

"You got any tattoos, Olga?" Nancy asked.

"Why?" Olga took a step backwards, placed her arse on a concrete block that she guessed was once a plinth for an urn or garden ornament.

"Just curious." Nancy smiled and sipped her drink.

"Only one."

"You have?" Spencer perched next to her, close, so close their legs and arms touched.

Olga swigged some more cider, four big gulps.

"Where?" Spencer nudged her with his shoulder.

"You really want to know?"

"Yes." He lowered his voice. "I told you, I want to know everything."

His now appley-breath washed over her. "On my leg."

His attention shifted downwards. "I can't see it, and I can see most of your legs."

"Yeah, where is it?" Nancy asked.

Olga shrugged and took another drink.

"I don't believe you," Charles said, tossing one can aside and opening another.

"Don't then." She huffed.

"Show me," Spencer said.

"Show all of us." Rebecca grinned. "You're the only one here brave enough to have a tattoo."

"Yeah, did it hurt?" Nancy asked.

"A bit." Olga shrugged.

"Go on, show us." Spencer did that thing again, pushed her hair behind her ear, his light touch, the brush of his fingers, making a rush of feathery sensation tickle over her scalp.

"Okay." She handed him her can, then stood straight. Already the booze had gone to her head, giving her a slightly floaty feeling, one she liked—it helped her forget. "It's here." She yanked at the base of her leather skirt, revealing more of the tatty fishnet stockings and beneath them the garter tattoo she'd had done the year before.

"Fuck, you weren't joking," Spencer said, his eyes widening.

"Why would I joke?" Joking wasn't something she usually did, but she supposed Spencer didn't know that about her yet.

"I love it." Nancy moved closer to inspect it.

Rebecca followed. "It could almost be real lace. Really clever."

Olga swelled with pride. She loved her tattoo, even though she'd had to hide it from her mother ever since she'd had it done. She took hold of the fishnets, ripped them a little more to reveal the ink better.

"Wow, and that's a…dagger stuffed in the garter." Nancy pointed at it. "The handle's great."

Olga shrugged. It was great. The artist had been a genius. The emerald-green handle sparkled, and there was a glint of light on the base of the dagger, which appeared to be held in place with the garter, so the blade looked metallic.

"The dagger is a bit…menacing," Spencer said, his attention fixed on it.

"Perhaps." She raised her eyebrows.

"What's it symbolise?" Charles asked. "All art should mean something. Or so Mrs Jackson says."

"And it is art." Spencer nodded. "Like, really fucking good art."

"It shows," Olga puffed up her chest, "that a woman can be feminine, wear lace garters and all that jazz, yet be deadly if crossed. She can switch from friend to enemy, lover to murderer in an instant. She's always ready to act."

"Deadly. Murderer." Charles laughed. "And lace garters. It's like something from the Wild West."

She pushed her skirt into place and frowned. She didn't like being laughed at.

"Well, I think it's lovely," Nancy said. "Though goodness knows how you got it done when you're weren't eighteen."

"I just said I was." That was the truth. With full Goth makeup on and being tall, she could easily pass as a few years older. And in a parlour where making money was the main aim, it hadn't been a problem. Saving up her pocket money had been the difficult bit of the whole secret project.

"I think it's hot," Spencer said, handing her can of drink back.

"Hot?"

"Yeah, like really fucking sexy."

She swallowed. Never in her wildest dreams had she ever thought Spencer Cambridge would call her hot and sexy. And now here he was, smiling at her, pupils wide, the setting sun casting shadows on his perfect features and making her feel crazy with the possibilities that lay ahead.

He clinked his can on hers. "Here's to me finding out much more about you. I get the feeling this has only just begun."

"Hear, hear," Nancy said. "Good to have you join the gang, Olga."

"I agree." Rebecca beamed up at her. "Here's to finishing college and discovering all that lies ahead in the big bad world."

Olga didn't know what to say. So she said nothing. Instead, she drained her can, crushed it, and tossed it to one side.

Charles stood, walked down the steps, and dipped into the cool box. "Here. Have another." He handed Olga a cold, damp can.

"Er, thanks. What do I owe you for these?"

"Nothing." He smiled. "Our treat. We wanted you here."

"Yes. We did." Spencer snaked his arm around her waist, holding her possessively, as if she belonged to him now.

It was a nice feeling, combined with the cider, the sunset, and having new friends.

Maybe life wasn't so bad. Maybe it could even be good.

The shadows extended. The conversation flittered from gossip about other friends, who was dating who, online tittle-tattle from Facebook and Instagram, an upcoming concert in the local town, holidays planned, and the rumour that Mr Kent, Olga's biology teacher, was screwing Miss Caron, the French teacher. Olga hoped he wasn't. She liked Mr Kent, he deserved someone nicer than that drippy cow who never ever smiled.

The Moorhouse fell into darkness, the glassless windows resembling big dark eyes and the doorway a gaping mouth.

Nancy lit several tealights in small white holders—very fancy—and put them around the place. They gave it a magical feel, and as Olga started on her fifth can, she leaned closer to Spencer, enjoying his body warmth.

Charles started telling some story about their dog chasing a cat. Nancy and Rebecca seemed engrossed. Olga couldn't tell if they fancied him or if they were all just friends as they claimed to be.

"I want to kiss you again," Spencer whispered beside her ear, his lips touching her flesh and his chest pushing up against her shoulder.

"What?" She spun to face him, the tip of her nose bumping his.

"You heard." He grinned. "I want to kiss you again. Once was not enough."

She swallowed. She was a bit woozy; she hoped her legs would work long enough to get her home. "Kiss me?"

"Yes, but not here." He nodded at the dark shell of The Moorhouse. "In there."

It was dark and creepy, but that didn't bother Olga. Hell, that was her comfort zone.

"Argh, there's a bat." Nancy squealed.

"It's only a Pipistrelle," Olga said, watching it dart away. "Tiny, hardly going to hurt you."

"It'll tangle in my hair." Nancy grabbed a cap and slapped it on her head, covering her long, silky blonde hair.

Charles laughed and hugged her. "I'll protect you."

"Yeah, right." She dug her elbow into him.

He reeled away, laughing, then lunged at her.

Nancy shrieked. Rebecca joined in the chaos. They became a tumbling threesome roll of arms and legs.

"Come on, let's leave them to it." Spencer pushed to standing and took hold of her hand. "While they're busy and don't notice us slipping away."

Olga looked at the house again. Inside it was empty and barren, she knew that. No furniture, just the cracks and chaos of nature taking over.

"We should have some privacy," Spencer said. "Away from these kids."

Nancy, Rebecca, and Charles were lost in some kind of wild tickling game, the cries of laughter getting louder.

She swigged back her cider, suppressed a burp, then took Spencer's hand. Was this really happening? Hell yeah.

She followed him to the house, up the steps, and through the dark doorway. Her lips tingled with the thought of kissing him again, feeling his mouth on hers, his tongue, too.

Spencer led her past a wonky old staircase that had several floorboards missing and a Virginia creeper growing up the bannister. The hilarity of the others faded. They went deeper into the house; it grew darker, until they reached the kitchen at the back.

Here the moonlight was spilling in through the broken windows. The huge silver disc had just risen from the dense patch of trees as it climbed into the sky. An owl hooted, or more like screamed; it was a juvenile.

"What the fuck was that?" Spencer said, glancing outside.

Olga giggled. "It's just a tawny owl. That's the noise they make when they're learning to twit-twoo properly." She hiccupped and put her fingers over her mouth.

He laughed then wrapped his arms around her waist, pushing her backwards until she hit a dusty old wooden table.

"Spencer, what are you doing?" She smiled and slung her arms over his shoulders, fastened her fingers at his nape. He was so tall, broad, too, and beneath his polo shirt his muscles were hard and strong.

"What do you think I'm doing?" He kissed her again, and she melted against him.

The next thing she knew he was undoing her blouse. Her brain was telling her to stop him, but her body wasn't listening.

She groaned softly, and the kiss intensified. Her blouse was off now, cool evening air washing over her bare skin. Then her bra was gone, too.

She trembled, anticipation like a real living thing inside her.

But Spencer didn't caress her. Instead, he shoved at her skirt, pushing that and her tights and knickers down, too.

"No, please."

"Hey, we can't have much fun with clothes on." He cupped her cheek and stared into her eyes. "It's just me and you, don't worry. There's no one else back here."

As he'd said that, a twig snapped outside. She stared at the window.

"Damn owl," he said, grinning then kissing her again.

Immediately she was lost to him. Her clothes were abandoned now, on the floor and sitting around her boots. He was breathing fast, so was she. He cupped her arse then spoke onto her lips. "Get on your knees. You taste me then I'll taste you."

He applied pressure to her shoulders, forced her to fold before him. And then he was fiddling with his belt buckle and the button on his jeans.

The cider swirled in her belly. Grit poked at her kneecaps. This wasn't quite as romantic as she'd hoped her first encounter with a bloke would be.

"Ah yeah, that's it, beautiful Olga. Let me see that sexy tongue piercing."

He cupped her chin and smiled at her.

She poked out her tongue.

A blinding flash attacked her. Then another. It filled her vision like a bolt of lightning.

"What the hell?" She stood, twisted to face the window.

Another white-hot flash.

A phone.

Taking pictures.

A wild cackle of laughter peeled around the kitchen. Girls.

And then a male voice. "Fucking hell, here was me thinking she'd have scales and green skin." Charles roared with laughter.

Another flash.

Olga slapped her right arm over her breasts, her left hand at the juncture of her thighs. "What the fucking hell are you doing?"

Spencer was laughing, tucking himself away. "You didn't really think we were going to do it, did you?"

She stared at him wide-eyed, confusion a slap to her face. She stepped backwards, behind the table. Stumbled when her clothing tangled in her boots. She lurched forward, her arse sticking in the air.

Another picture.

"You fucking bastard, Spencer," she snarled, finally making it to the semi-safety of the back of the kitchen and hiding behind the table and a tall chair. "You set me up."

"You set yourself up." Charles chuckled. The outline of his head was at the window, Nancy and Rebecca either side. "A few messages, a few ciders, and you thought Spencer Cambridge had fallen in love with you."

"A freak like you," Nancy said, then reeled with hysterical laughing. "Oh my God, this is the funniest thing ever."

"Let's look at the pictures." Rebecca's face lit up as she studied her screen. "Oh Jesus on a bike, they're better than we could have hoped. She's so super fucking ridiculous."

"Delete them. Now!" Olga was dragging at her clothes.

"What, and spoil all our fun?" Spencer said, running his hand through his hair.

Olga lunged at him, slapping his face, punching his chest, his stomach. She rained as many hits down on him as she could. Which wasn't many. He was taller than her, much stronger, and he pushed her away. "Get a grip, Goth-freak. Next time you'll stick to your own weirdo group of friends."

"I'm going to post this one on Facebook now," Rebecca said. "It's the perfect humiliation shot." She spun the phone around.

Olga was at a distance, but she could still see that it was her, naked but for her clothes bunched around her boots, mouth a perfect 'O' of surprise, eyes wide and the tattoo she kept hidden on full view. "Don't. Please."

"I can do what I want. This is my phone, a picture I took. I own the copyright." She cackled louder.

"Yeah, do it," Charles said. "And I'll post mine, too."

"Charles, please, no. I'm begging you."

"Why should I do what you want me to?" Charles laughed.

"Because if you do put that online," Olga was struggling not to puke, "I swear, it will be the last post you ever make."

"Why?" Nancy snarled, all her prettiness draining away in an instant. "What are you gonna do to stop us?"

"I'll fucking kill you, bitch." Olga swung her gaze to Charles then Rebecca. "And you, too." She spun to Spencer who was standing feet hip width apart, hands jammed onto his waist. "And you, you lying, shit-face wanker, I'll cut your cock off and shove it in your mouth until you choke to death on it."

"Yeah, yeah, I'd like to see you try." He chuckled. "Come on, you guys. Let's get some more cider then sit and see what comments we get. This is going to be classic."

Chapter Five

Shona shoved the wrapper from her morning muesli bar into the side compartment on her car door and pulled into a parking space near Ironash High Street. She'd called Earle on the way, told him she'd be a little late into the station that morning.

She headed into the centre of town, glad of her thin cotton navy trousers and matching blouse. It was going to be another hot day, which was good for all the music festivalgoers. Today was the first day of the three-day event which promised lots of hits, hippies, and happiness. Shona couldn't see the appeal of camping, that really wasn't her thing. But the music she would enjoy, if she got the chance to visit the festival. The line-up was pretty decent.

Frasers, a department store that had been in Ironash forever, was situated on the corner of High Street and Burn End. She went through the revolving doors. Instantly, the cacophony of scents from the perfume section swirled around her. Which was good, smells were what she'd come for.

She tightened her handbag over her shoulder and walked up to the first desk she saw—men's aftershave and cologne. The bottles were all dark, exotic colours, and posters of handsome actors and sportsmen were dotted about—blokes she guessed regular men wanted to emulate.

Black Noir. She picked it up, sprayed it into the air. Sniffed. No, it wasn't that one. Roman Power. She did the same, the mist catching in the light pouring in through a window to her left. Nope, definitely not, it was way too fruity. She was hunting for a rich, spiced, almost incense-like scent. She repeated the process with Night Hunter.

"Can I help you?" a sales assistant, tall, thin, pale, and with dazzling pink lipstick asked.

"No, I'm okay, thanks." Shona picked up Homme and sprayed.

"Here. Here. Use this." The assistant handed her a white strip of paper. "Spray on the end, it's easier."

"Okay, thanks." She did just that. Sniffed. No, this one was too fresh, like open water.

"Are you looking for something in particular?"

"Kind of."

"Do you know the name of it?"

"No, that's the problem." Divine Inspiration, perhaps that was it. She sprayed onto the opposite end of the paper. Nope, not that one, too citrusy, she placed it down next to a small glossy black Buddha ornament. "Can I have some more of these?" She held up the strip.

A moment of hesitation then, "Of course. Here you go." She handed one over.

"I don't think that's quite going to cut it. I need several."

Several were produced, wordlessly.

Shona stepped away, spotted Road Rebel, and tried that. Nope. Silent Type. Not that one either. Tutting, she moved to the next counter which luckily didn't seem to be manned by a sales assistant.

She started to work her way through more male colognes. It had to be one of them, surely. Even more so if the Asian was from Ironash, which her gut instinct was telling her he was.

Wild Card was too heavy, Packed, too light. Branded could have been the one, maybe, so she set it aside.

"Excuse me, are you sure I can't help you with something?" It was the sales assistant again.

"I'm trying to find a cologne with a thick spice smell." Shona sighed. "I'm not getting very far, though."

"I see, you like, or the man in your life, he likes notes of pepper, cardamom, paprika."

"Er, yes, that's right."

"Mmm." She appeared happy to have a task. "Let's see." With a flourish of energy, she picked up a shiny black bottle. "Try this."

"I have, it's not that one."

"Oh. Okay." She frowned. "Well how about Damage? That's heavy."

"Let me try it." Shona took it, found a patch of paper to spray it on. She closed her eyes, inhaled. It was definitely spicy below the alcohol. But was it the spiced scent from her memory? No. It really wasn't.

She held in a frustrated sigh. "No. Not this one."

"I'm afraid, madam, you have tried all of the most popular aftershaves. Firm favourite classics and new releases."

"Really, all of them? New and old?" She held up her handful of white paper sticks.

"Yes. Maybe you'll have more luck in our bigger branch, in Manchester, if you can't find what you're looking for."

Shona got the distinct impression she was being dismissed. It irked her, that did. "There's that shelf over there. I can see a few I haven't tested."

"Excuse me, miss, can I pay for these?"

The sales assistant glanced at the customer to her left. "I'll be with you in a moment." She turned back to Shona. "They have a much larger selection in Manchester." She held out her hand. "Shall I take those for you, so you don't have to find a bin on High Street?"

What the hell? Shona hadn't finished yet. She had no intention of going onto High Street. So she did something she'd never done before in a shop. She flipped open her bag and pulled out her ID.

The sales assistant's eyes bugged. "Oh, you're a...?"

"Police detective, yes, and the reason I'm smelling these colognes here is because I'm working on a very important, top secret case, and I can't tell you any more than that."

"Oh, really. Does one of the criminals wear a scent?" She rubbed her hands together, and a sparkle caught in her eye. "I'm sure you're right, it would be heavy and strong, or at least that's what I'd imagine a baddie to wear." She scooted to her right, picked up a purple bottle with an orange stripe going over it. "This. It's horrible, likely to be just the sort lowlife scum would choose."

"Miss, please, I have to get to work, can I pay for this here?"

"No, sorry." The sales assistant tilted her chin. "I'm doing some important undercover police work." She sidled nearer to Shona and lowered her voice. "I haven't given too much away, have I?"

"No, that's okay." Shona held in a smile.

"Police work?" the customer said with a frown.

"Yes, super important, life and death actually, so you'll have to go and pay at the main till."

"But it will only take a—"

"Life or death." The sales assistant waggled her finger. "Go and pay over there."

The customer tutted and walked off.

"Now, Officer, try this."

Shona stepped back as the air between her and the sales assistant filled with damp spray. She sniffed warily.

It really was a gross aftershave. Heavy and thick, it reminded her of wet dogs. "Oh no, nasty, but it's not the one." She peered at the shelf. "Any other ideas?"

"Mmm, yes, this one."

Another spray. Another light scent. Nothing spiced about it.

The next one caught Shona's attention, and she stepped away, eyes closed, sniffing the paper. It had a note of nutmeg but it was too musky. Not quite right.

She sighed and checked her watch. She had to get going.

"What about this one." The sales assistant handed over another bottle. Emerald green, it was called Wizard.

"Worth a try." Shona smelled it. Vanilla, pine woods, cedar. "No, not that one. Sorry." She rummaged for her car keys. "Thank you, though—"

"Shelly. Shelly Bright."

"Thank you, Shelly. You've been most helpful."

"Always happy to help the law." She did a mock salute. "I hope you catch the bad guys and if I can do anything else to help, let me know."

"Thanks." Shona smiled. "I appreciate that."

But driving to Ironash Police Station, she was disheartened. She'd sniffed so many colognes she had a headache and still hadn't come near to what she was searching for. Everything was too refined, too tinged with the alcohol base. And would they stay as strong as she remembered it to be, once applied and a few hours had passed? The smell during the attack was one of her most vivid recollections.

There was only one thing for it. She'd have to keep looking...or rather sniffing.

"Hey, Earle," she said, arriving at her desk next to his. "All okay?"

"Define okay?"

"No one dead."

"Yep, all is okay then."

"Good." She sat. "This place is quiet."

"The festival."

"Ah, yes, I forgot. Fletcher there, too?"

"No, he's at the dentist. Lost a crown while eating lasagne last night."

"Fun." She brought her computer to life. It suited her for Fletcher to be out for a while. While it was warming up, she called Barry Grey.

"Hello, Detective, what can I help you with?"

"Hi, Mr Grey."

"Barry, please."

"Barry. I wondered if I could book you for another sketch."

Earle glanced her way.

She ignored him.

"Yes, of course, only it will have to be after the weekend, I'm in Blackpool, visiting family."

"Oh, okay." She pushed down the disappointment in her voice. "Monday then?"

"Perfect, evening again?"

"Yes, I'll drop you a text to confirm. Can never quite tell if I'll get off duty on time."

"I understand. See you then."

She ended the call.

"He's a good bloke, Barry," Earle said.

"Yes, he is."

"You get what you needed last time?" His attention flicked to her drawer.

"Yes, thank you." She clicked her mouse and went to old records. She put in the date of her attack.

"Andy's in today," Earle said.

"Andy?"

"Yes, you met him on your first day, he's our man. Anything you need, old files, technical stuff, ANPR, CCTV, just shout, he'll be on it."

"Cool." She glanced over at Andy. He was young, with blond hair. Currently he was staring intently between two computer screens. "His father-in-law just died, didn't he?"

"Yes, he's got the funeral tomorrow but said he wanted to be here today, keep his mind off things."

"Can't blame him. Distraction is excellent therapy."

"Want a coffee?"

"Please."

Earle unfolded to his full height and wandered off.

Shona opened the file. It was pitifully small despite there being three victims. Evidence was sparse.

She started reading. Her throat tightened, and a rush of adrenaline mixed with anger shot into her blood stream. But she kept her cool. It was the only way to get answers.

She skimmed over the personal details of herself, Tina, and Nicola—she knew them—and went to the evidence. There were no solid witnesses. The girls had been drugged, their memories of the event virtually non-existent.

Opening the photograph file, she looked over at Earle. He was chatting to Darren from the front desk and waiting for the kettle to boil.

"Be strong," she muttered and opened her own file. Pictures of her in a hospital gown. Her wrists and ankles bruised and red, a mark around her throat. Vacant eyes wide with dark circles around them. She clenched her fists; the need to punch something was acute. Could she hang on until karate later? She'd have to.

She clicked on Nicola's pictures. Same vacant expression, she had the added bonus of a black eye. This time Shona had to fight back a sudden prickle of tears on her lower lids. God, she missed that sweet, sweet girl. She'd been broken on the outside, but totally destroyed on the inside by the events of that night. It seemed the not knowing was as brutal as knowing. Imagination was a bastard, that was one thing she knew.

Tina's pictures were much the same. She had a cut on her lip, and her eyes were closed, her hands clasped. Shona remembered she'd been shaking when they'd been found. She hadn't stopped the whole time they'd been at the station and with the doctor and detectives.

She went deeper into the file, sought out the forensic report. Nothing had been found on her or Tina's body. They'd all been showered before being dumped naked on Six Mile Lane. But beneath Nicola's fingernails, DNA was discovered. The DNA of her attacker.

Trouble was, the report stated that it was unidentified. Not on the database. This wasn't new to Shona, the police had told her and her family that at the time. But seeing it now, it rammed home how cunning and calculated the three men had been.

Time had passed, though. Maybe this arsehole was on the database now. She'd run a check.

Earle appeared.

She closed the file.

He set a mug of coffee beside her keyboard.

"Thanks."

He sighed and plonked himself down.

"What's up?" she asked, reaching for her drink. Perhaps it would get rid of the thud in her temples.

"Tammy?"

"Tammy?"

"Yeah, you know. Short-shorts, garden gnomes."

"Ah, yes. *That* Tammy." Shona pressed her lips together to hold in a smile. Tammy had the hots for Earle. Shona didn't need to have detective training to know that. "What about her?"

"She's just called the front desk. Seems there's been another gnome robbery from her mother's garden."

Shona shrugged. "A crime is a crime and needs investigating."

He appeared crestfallen.

"Send a uniform," she said with a chuckle. "We've got other stuff to do."

"They're all at the festival. We're the only ones free apparently."

She laughed a little more at the misery in his voice. "We could leave it until next week, but I reckon we should view it as a bit of light relief after investigating three murders in quick succession. A gnome kidnap isn't so high octane."

Earle muttered something, gulped his coffee, and stood. "In that case, we should get this over and done with."

Chapter Six

Earle drove them to Tammy's mother's house. She lived on the Wilton Estate, near the canal.

He was quiet. His phone rang once, a private number. He didn't accept the call.

Shona didn't comment.

When they pulled against the kerb outside their destination, an ice cream van was parked up. A gaggle of children were queuing beside it, coins clutched in their palms as they chattered excitedly.

"Want one?" she said.

"Yeah, I might actually."

They wandered over. A net curtain twitched in a house to their right. Nosey neighbours were good news for police officers, a sure supply of information when something untoward occurred.

After waiting a couple of minutes they bought a Mr Whippy each. Earle opted for a Flake. Shona gave chocolate a miss.

Standing near the car, the kids scattering, they ate.

"You heard from your old partner?" Shona asked. "What was his name?"

"Patrick, and no, why would I?"

His stiff reaction surprised her. "I just presumed you'd been friends as well as colleagues."

He studied her through narrowed eyes. Silence.

"That he might have let you know how his new position is going. He went north, right?"

Earle crunched into his cone. Chewed. Swallowed. "You have a good memory."

"It's my job." She shrugged and licked her ice cream. "How long did you work together?"

"Nearly two years." Clipped response.

"So you weren't mates, outside of work?"

"No." He stepped away. "Come on, let's get this over with."

He walked off, his long legs moving quickly and covering the ground with swift efficiency.

Shona followed him, shoving in the last of her ice cream and trying to dampen down her curiosity. What was it with Earle's old partner? He certainly didn't like talking about him. Had they fallen out, their relationship turned sour?

Earle waited until she stood beside him, then rang the doorbell. She brushed a crumb from her blouse.

The door pulled open.

Tammy stood there smiling broadly, her attention firmly on Earle. It was as though Shona didn't exist. Her curly brown hair was loose and fell around her slim shoulders. Like before, her long tanned legs were shown off by denim shorts, but today she'd teamed them with a pink t-shirt. A waft of flowery perfume encircled her. "Detective Montague, it's so good to see you. Thank you for coming around so quickly. My mother is quite distraught that another gnome has gone. She's very fond of them all. They each have a name, individual personalities, to her at least."

Shona glanced at the front garden. There were a total of eight gnomes set around the flowerpots and shrubs. Some were fishing in piles of pebbles, some had hands on hips grinning, and one was flashing his round pink bottom.

"I know it's not crime of the century," Tammy went on. "And what with the awful things on the news this week, that poor old dear whose house burnt down and then that man and..." She tutted and shook her head. "Anyway, do come in, don't stand there. I'll get you a drink, you must be so hot, this weather again. What a summer we're having, right." She grinned, gesturing for them to enter the house.

Earle gave a tight sigh and stepped inside. His fists were in tight balls.

Shona tailed him.

They walked past a staircase and a closed door then entered a kitchen. It led out onto a sunny back garden with a large patio area. Many more gnomes were set amongst the greenery.

"Mum is out there. Her hearing aid is turned on." Tammy nodded. "Go see her, and I'll get the drinks. Lemonade okay?"

"Perfect, thank you." Shona looked about. It was a nice house, with a nice atmosphere, as though it was filled with happy memories and they'd seeped into the very fabric of the walls, floors, and ceilings.

They went outside. Tammy's mother was sitting under a red parasol that in turn made her glow red.

"Hello, Mrs Robin," Shona said. "I'm DI Williams, and this is DS Montague. We're here about the missing gnome."

The old lady's eyebrows rose. "You are?"

"Yes." Earle took out his notepad.

"I didn't expect the police to be interested in my gnomes."

Tammy walked out, holding a tray. "I called them, Mum. You can't let thieves get away with taking what's not theirs."

"I suppose." Mrs Robin shrugged. "But I'm not too worried, Officers, it's not as if I can't spare a few of the little fellas." She nodded at the garden. "I bought one, years ago, and said I loved his cheeky face, and since then, that's all my family ever buy me for Christmas and birthdays." She huffed. "I probably should be grateful they remember but…well…you can have too much of a good thing."

"Mum!" Tammy said, her eyes widening. "I thought you loved getting gnomes."

"I do. I do, but…" She sighed. "Some slippers or hand cream would be nice, too."

Tammy turned from her mother. Her eyes were a little misted, and she blinked rapidly a few times. Silently, she handed Earle a tumbler of lemonade.

"Thank you," he said, shifting from one foot to the other.

"So really, Officers, I don't want you to waste your precious time on this matter." Mrs Robin wafted a small fly away.

"You don't want to officially report it as a crime?" Shona asked, taking the drink she was offered.

"Oh no, not at all."

"Or press charges if we catch the culprit?" She sipped the cloudy lemonade. Delicious.

"I haven't got the energy for that kind of thing. I'm eighty-three, dear. Besides, I'm sure you kind folk will give him a slap on the wrist for me, if you ever catch the thief."

"We will certainly have a stern word." Earle flipped his notebook closed and tucked it into his pocket. He downed his lemonade and set it back on the tray Tammy was still holding.

Tammy pulled in a deep breath and seemed to compose herself. "I'm sorry to waste your time, Officer Montague. Really I am. It's the last thing I'd want to do."

"Not a problem." He smiled at her.

"And we were glad of the drink. Very nice by the way." Shona returned her glass.

"Thank you. I made it myself." Tammy batted her eyelashes at Earle. "I adore homemade things, lemonade, cakes, jams, pickles, anything really. I love to cook. I love to care for people, feed them, make them happy."

"That's nice." Earle stepped past her, towards the house.

"I have some bread baking, if you need lunch," she said, scooting after him.

"Goodbye, Mrs Robin, have a nice day." Shona smiled.

"Goodbye, dear."

In the kitchen, Tammy had cornered Earle beside the oven. "Can you smell it, Officer? It's got sesame oil in it, makes it extra nice, like that tiger bread at Tesco, you know."

"Very good." He glanced at his watch. "We really have to go."

"Oh yes, of course, silly me. It's the music festival, isn't it. Must keep you busy, all those extra people in town." She pushed her hair over her shoulders, fluttered her eyelashes. "I might just go myself later. I love a bit of a dance. Is that where you'll be?"

"Yes, most likely," Shona said. "Perhaps we'll see you there."

Tammy kept her attention glued on Earle. "I really hope so." She grinned, her glossy red lips stretching wide as she pressed her hand over her chest.

"We have to go." Earle moved into the corridor.

Shona glanced after him. "Sorry to rush off, Miss Robin, we've—"

"He's busy, you're busy, I know." There was longing in her voice. "Do you think...?"

"What?"

She lowered her voice. "He's single, right? Officer Montague."

"I wouldn't like to comment on that." Shona downturned her mouth. "Sorry." She had to stay professional.

"Well, I'm pretty sure he is, I've asked around see, and...do you think...?"

Shona waited for her to go on.

"Do you think he likes me?" She paused. "Like in *that* way?"

Tammy clearly had a major crush going on. And it was hardly a surprise. Earle was a great-looking man, and he definitely had that certain something that had women's heads turning. ""What's not to like, Tammy, you're a very attractive woman."

"Thank you." She sighed. "I just wish I could read him, figure out if he likes me, too. I'm usually pretty good at that, but Earle...Officer Montague, well, I'm stuck."

"Maybe you'll just have to ask him. Come out with it."

"But when?" Tammy nibbled on her bottom lip. "Perhaps at the music festival, eh?" She nodded. "Yes, I'll get myself down there. Just...you know, say it. Ask him. Right out."

"Seems you have a plan."

Shona said goodbye and joined Earle in the car. He'd turned the engine and air-conditioning on. She was glad of it and quickly slammed the door shut to retain the cool.

"She likes you, Earle."

He huffed.

"She's nice, fun, pretty, too, don't you think?"

"I'm sure she is. Fun, that is."

"So you don't think she's pretty?"

"I haven't thought about it. Why would I?"

"Well, only that you're a single man, she's a single woman who's obviously into you. I just presumed—"

"Well don't. Presume, I mean."

"Hey, okay." Shona held up her hands. "I was only saying."

He gripped the steering wheel with both hands and stared at the road ahead.

"I'm sorry," Shona said, wishing she'd kept her mouth shut. The tension in the car was electric. The tiny hairs on her forearms were tingling. "For mentioning it, it's none of my business, you're right."

"No, it's not," he snapped.

She swallowed tightly, holding in a retort.

"Fuck, I'm sorry." He squeezed the bridge of his nose and closed his eyes.

"No, it's me who should be sorry. We haven't been working together long. The last thing I want is tension between us. I was in the wrong."

"What you said and thought was perfectly natural, but..."

"But?"

He set his attention on Shona, his dark eyes unblinking, his jaw set tight.

She fought what she knew was an expression of surprise. "Ah, okay."

"Have I shocked you?"

"Er, no...not at all."

"Some people are. It's why I...don't advertise."

She reached over and touched his thick, corded forearm. "I've got your back." A little niggle of doubt needled her. Was that the right thing to say? "What I mean is, I like to keep my private life private, too. We all have secrets, right?"

He nodded. "Yep, even the good guys have secrets."

Chapter Seven

Olga hadn't intended to go to Ironash Festival, but when she'd spotted on Facebook that the four Devil's spawn were going, she'd sold a couple of rare vinyls and splashed out on a ticket.

Her mother was in a bad way, after two weeks of calm—the calm before the storm. A black mood had moved like a glacier carving through her mania and grinding down every emotion that wasn't deathly and dark. Normally Olga wouldn't have left her in what was her own personal version of Hell, but this time, she'd had no choice.

There were things to do.

She banged a tent peg into the ground, wishing it were Spencer's face she was driving it into—eyes, nostrils, throat, it didn't matter.

The pain of the social media posts was still so raw. 'Time healed' people said, but not for Olga. Each passing minute without vengeance added to the agony. It twisted and curled around her soul, squeezing out her breath, destroying her very life force. Soon she'd be dead because of it. A wisp of air. A shadow of who she once was.

Reaching for another peg, Olga found that a memory of one of the Facebook posts flitted unwantedly into her brain. It accompanied the picture of her trying to cover her nakedness when she'd realised what was happening. Rebecca, the bitch, had added...

News Flash—Goths don't have green skin and scales, just flab, gross big tits, and hideous tattoos!

Olga whacked the tent peg. This time she wished she was whacking Rebecca's skull with the mallet, watching it cave inwards, brain and goo bulging out.

The post had been liked by over six hundred people—six fucking hundred. Who even had that many friends?

Olga held back a now familiar swell of nausea.

The comments were almost as humiliating as the picture. Some from names she recognised, but most of them she didn't.

Can't be unseen!!!!!!

I just threw up my breakfast—green face emoji.

How do you get a Goth down from a tree? Cut the rope. HAHAHAHA

She should go and kill herself now—skull emoji.

Bitch is a freak.

Put a bag over her head, I'd fuck her—actually no, not even then. Vom!

The tent peg sank into the earth, grass covering the tip. Olga wiped her forearm over her brow. She'd reported it to Facebook. Had never heard back. So everything was still there. For everyone to see. For all of time. Forever.

She tightened the next string, set to securing it to the ground. The spot she'd picked was away from the main crowd of brightly coloured and patterned tents. She'd opted for a location behind a stack of straw bales and looking down over the long row of Portaloos and temporary shower block. She was near to a wooden fence, new, and over that was the pinewoods. She hoped no one would tell her to move her small, domed black tent. Not now it was up.

She liked the density of the trees and the privacy the straw bales gave her. She didn't care that she couldn't see the stage or that she wasn't part of the action—she was going to make her own action.

With the tent secure, she crawled in and set about organising the supplies in her backpack.

She'd brought tins and packets of food—eating at the burger van was expensive—and had lugged two big bottles of water over the field with all the rest of her stuff. She set her food out in a neat row. Next she folded her spare clothes and put them in a pile. Two fresh t-shirts—Skeletal Family and Alien Sex Fiend—long skirt, black jeans, a hoody she'd tie-dyed purple, and another old Iron Maiden one. They'd be important, the fresh clothes, as would the black bin liners she added beside them.

She spread out her roll mat—it was actually a yoga mat her mother had bought during a manic episode when she'd decided that was to be her new hobby. Of course she'd only tried it once, for half an hour, then declared it a waste of time. But that mat would be better than just the hard ground for a bed, and Olga spread her sleeping bag over it and added a thin pillow.

After checking the zip on her tent was drawn down tight, she took out her latest creations.

Spencer. Charles. Rebecca. Nancy.

Small dolls made from a sponge and scraps of material. Each fashioned to represent her four tormentors.

Her four victims.

Olga refused to be a victim. That wasn't how this was going to end.

Fat and ugly. Should be burned alive—flame emoji.

Satan worshipper!

I bet 'it' drinks blood for breakfast—vampire GIF

Slut needs the weird fucked out of her—but not by me!

She inhaled deeply. In the distance, a warm-up band crashed out its first track. She welcomed the noise; it dulled the screaming in her head.

Spencer's little drawn-on face stared at her. His blond hair stuck up, and his mouth was a simple straight red line.

Olga held a pin over his face. She slid it into his right eye, slowly, enjoying the ride of sharp metal through soft sponge.

She took another pin, held it over his groin. "You'll pay for what you did." She pushed it in, imagining it going through his cock. Oh, how he'd scream.

Or at least she hoped he would.

Next came Charles. Olga hated Charles with an intensity that scared her. His wicked actions, his evil pre-empted plotting to take pictures of her with his brother meant he, too, deserved what he got.

This time she reached for a pair of scissors, steel, long and strong. Charles was the same as Spencer in doll form, except he had a blue top on instead of red.

Proof that Goths don't just worship the Devil #gothonherknees

Charles' post had been accompanied with a shocking image of Olga near naked and kneeling in front of Spencer, looking for all the world like she was giving him a blow job. Spencer's face had, of course, been blurred out. But every detail of Olga was clear to see—round white arse, scrappy green-tipped hair, the spots on the backs of her arms that would never go away.

Bitch needs to stay down there LOL

Suck it up!

Braver man than me #Ilikemydick

Olga snipped off first the right, then the left of the Charles doll's hands. If the real Charles hadn't had hands, then he wouldn't have been able to take the picture and he wouldn't have been able to type out that post.

Fuck, will it bleed a lot? When I chop off his hands?

Olga smiled. So what if it did?

Next came Nancy. Proof that a pretty face didn't make for a pretty soul. Nancy was the Devil wrapped up in blonde hair and long fluttery lashes. She didn't know what Spencer saw in her, but it was clear that was where his affections lay, and always had.

You are a stupid cow, Olga, thinking for even a minute he liked you.

Olga had beaten herself up until her emotions were black and blue. Her cider-swilling, guard-down ways of that fateful night had been her undoing. Trusting another human being was a big mistake she'd only ever make once.

She poked the end of the scissors onto the Nancy doll's face. Pressed hard, harder still, and then opened them, the sharp pointy ends tearing the material so the sponge beneath was revealed.

If bitch Nancy hadn't had a mouth, she wouldn't have been able to convince Olga that she was welcome in their group. If she hadn't smiled, laughed, drawn Olga in as though she were nothing more than a stupid moth being attracted to a candle, this wouldn't have happened.

Nancy would pay for her deceit. She'd pay the ultimate price. Olga would see to that.

She turned her attention to Rebecca. Sweet little Rebecca, or so everyone thought. The hussy was in cahoots with the Devil. Like Nancy, she fooled people into thinking she was a truthful, fine, upstanding person, yet beneath the façade was a soul filled with black boiling swill, malicious intentions, a foulness that could never be eradicated.

But Rebecca could be eradicated.

And Olga intended to do just that.

With one quick snip, she took off the doll's head. It landed on Olga's voluminous black skirt, still smiling.

"Won't be smiling when it's for real, will you." Olga chuckled, enjoying the relief of stress and the way the sound coincided with the crescendo coming from the distant stage.

When twilight stretched its long, silken fingers over the fields and woods, Olga emerged from her tent. She'd kohled her eyes darker than ever before. Her skin was powdered ghostly white and her hair backcombed to within an inch of its life.

As she walked over the grass, past the straw bales and the Portaloos, she searched for section A4. Her victims had revealed on Facebook that was where their tents were. How easy it was to track them. Child's play. Laughable.

Olga chuckled as she spotted the handwritten sign for A4.

A popular band was playing. Most people were down by the stage. Only a few lingered around the tents. Several fires had been lit, the odd barbecue, too.

Olga moved silently, her skirt swishing around her legs, the sleeves of her tie-dyed hoody pulled down over her hands, concealing the long steel carving knife that pressed against her forearm.

The duct tape, she didn't conceal, she wore it like a bangle. She was weird. A freak. No one would question it.

Someone was throwing up. Nosily. Burping as he retched. Too much beer in the sunshine. Idiot.

Olga was stone-cold sober. She hadn't touched a drop since that night. Clearly alcohol wasn't for her. Cider had encouraged her to drop her guard and allowed someone to trick her. Never again.

She carried on, head down, but still taking in her surroundings. Her heart was thudding. Where were her victims? Rebecca had posted that her tent was covered in love hearts—puke—and easy to spot.

After pausing, checking out the surrounding tents, Olga carried on. It was then she spotted it. The stupid red-and-pink tent Rebecca had waffled on about on Facebook.

Olga's stomach clenched. A shot of adrenaline burst into her bloodstream. This was it. This was the moment she'd been dreaming of. Now all she had to do was wait.

She perched on a log someone had dragged over to use as a seat. Beside the love heart tent was a plain blue one, set at an angle to show they were together. Were Charles and Rebecca sharing? Nancy and Spencer? Of course they were. And these girls had the nerve to call her a slut. They were grade-A tarts. Whores.

The drummer was really going for it, slamming out a solo and vibrating the ground, shaking the soles of Olga's feet even through thick boots.

She touched the tip of her finger to the blade. It was dangerously sharp. A fraction more pressure, and she'd draw her own blood, which she might, if she had to endure this crap music for much longer.

Do people really like this shit?

It was then, in her peripheral vision, she saw him staggering between the tents and lurching her way.

Spencer.

Or was it Charles?

She kept her head low, strained her eyeballs to look.

Spencer.

It was definitely Spencer. His face was longer, his chin a tiny bit pointed.

She froze. The last thing she wanted was for him to see her…not yet anyway.

He burped loudly and clutched his stomach. He was staring at his feet as he listed left and right, bumped into a tent pole then tripped over a guide rope.

The drummer carried on his wild solo, upping the tempo to a frantic beat.

Spencer hauled himself up, finally reached the blue tent, next to the love heart monstrosity, and half fell, half crawled inside.

Olga glanced around. Where were the others? They were joined at the hip. Why was Spencer alone?

She stood, craned her neck to see over the spread of tents.

No Charles. No Rebecca. No Nancy.

A smile tugged her lips. It extended, balling her cheeks. It was the first smile since *that* night.

Chapter Eight

"I'd hoped to hit the festival?" Shona checked her watch. "But it's getting late? The Campbell paperwork has taken all afternoon."

"We still could, though." Earl stood from his desk and stretched his arms over his head, unravelling the knots in his spine. His fingertips almost touched the ceiling. "Unless you have something planned?"

"I was hoping to get some exercise in, but no worries, let's swing by, check out the lay of the land. I'd feel better if we did."

"I agree. It's quite an influx for the weekend. Has got bigger every year since it started four summers ago."

"Multiplied our usual population."

"Considerably." Earle picked up his car keys and dropped his phone and notebook into his back trouser pocket. "Makes me glad I'm not a uniform anymore."

"Me, too." She stood and grabbed her small bag. "Been there, done that."

"Shall we drive separately? So we can head for home...or the gym if you're that way inclined."

"Good plan."

"I can't believe you have the energy."

"It'll help me to unwind."

"Each to their own. For me, I'll hit the kitchen."

She laughed. "Baking again?"

"Why is that funny?"

"It's not." She straightened her face. "I think it's nice."

"You be careful or you won't get a slice of Darren's birthday cake tomorrow."

"Ohh, a birthday cake. What are you making?"

"Red velvet."

"My favourite."

"I'll remember that."

Her mouth watered. She'd never had a partner who could bake before and she wasn't complaining.

Shona followed along behind Earle, heading out of the town towards Downings Farm where the festival was held. As she neared, the lanes became cluttered with stationary empty vehicles, and a stubble field was bursting with parked cars. Ahead the huge stage was set on the slight rise of a hill, the crowd jostling around it—a sea of music fans. It wasn't dark yet; the sun was just kissing the tips of a stretch of woodland, long shadows spilling over the meadow chock full of small brightly coloured tents.

She drew to a halt, flashed her ID at the hired security, then pulled into a small section of grass cluttered with police vehicles and generators.

"Wow, it's loud," she said, joining Earle.

"Good band, though, don't you think?"

She listened for a moment. "Yeah, I've heard this song before."

"Shall we head for the central control tent?"

"Yes, where is it?"

"Last year it was beside the catering section."

"Makes sense."

Shona walked through the milling fans on the outskirts of the crowd. To her right the tents extended up the surrounding hills. Not much was going on there, seemed too much fun was to be had by the stage.

Earle had the effect of shifting people out of his way just by his presence. His height and width registering with folk at first glance, combined with his no-nonsense expression, he didn't need to advertise that he was a police officer to command respect and obedience.

They found the central control tent and went inside. Several uniforms were hanging about, sipping coffee, taking a break.

"All okay?" Shona asked, glancing at a map of the fields and adjacent area spread out on a table. There was a lot of farmland and woods, and it was a good distance from the town and other inhabitants. The music would hopefully only disturb a few owls, squirrels, and the odd deer.

"DI Williams, I presume." A smart young female officer smiled up from where she sat by a computer.

"Yes." Shona returned the smile.

"Welcome, I'm Sergeant Nicols. I'm coordinating this shift."

"Pleasure. Any incidents?"

"A few have been struck by sun and beer disease. A couple of minor scuffles but mostly quiet. It's early yet, though."

"Oh, you'll be in trouble for saying the 'Q' word." Earle laughed and helped himself to a coffee.

"It's never going to be quiet in the true sense," Nicols said. "The speakers are pointed this way, I swear." She rubbed her ears.

"It is loud. I like this band, though." Shona looked around. "How many uniforms have you got?"

"Forty, doing twelve-hour shifts each. Can get more if we need them."

"That's not many." Shona was shocked. She was used to many more.

"The hired help are doing a good job, professional company. Saves us manpower."

"True." Shona nodded. "I'll write my number down, though. Anything happens other than a minor scuffle, let me know." This was her patch now. The festival was a big deal, and she didn't want to find out when sitting at her desk the next morning that something major had occurred.

"Yes, ma'am." Nicols took the number and added it into her phone.

"Any time, okay," Shona said.

"You sure?"

"Absolutely." Ironash could be a dangerous place. Shona knew that only too well. And booze, music, and a huge crowd of youngsters could go from the best time ever to a major shitstorm in minutes. They were unpredictable, volatile, high on being together, and for some of them away from parental control for the first time.

"It'll be okay." Earle squeezed her shoulder. "They seem like good kids."

She had no idea how he'd come up with that impression from one walk through the crowd. But maybe that was just the cynic in her. She eyed people with suspicion these days. Earle would, too...eventually.

They headed outside. The same band was still on stage, a new drum-heavy tune ringing out. The crowd was a mix of ages, from teens to twenties and thirties.

She scanned faces, absorbed the atmosphere, getting a feel for the place. After twenty minutes her stomach rumbled. It had been a long time since she'd last eaten.

"What do you think?" She looked at her watch. "Time to go?"

"Yeah, they're under control here." Earle nodded. "Come on." He turned back the way they'd come.

It was then Shona saw him.

She was sure it was him.

The Asian from her drugged memory. The man she now had a sketch of.

Her heart did a weird flip then seemed to flop against her ribcage. Her belly tightened, sending a rush of nausea up her gullet. And a weird buzzing rang in her ears.

She stopped. Stared.

It was the thick eyebrow, almost one long line, and the shape of his jaw.

He was talking to another man who had his back to Shona.

"Fuck," she muttered. Much as she'd been on the hunt for this bloke, she hadn't expected to bump into him on a sunny evening at a music festival.

But then again...perhaps *he* was on the hunt.

She veered away from Earle, stomping over the grass.

He can't get away. I have to get to him.
And then what?
She had no evidence. Nothing to bring him in on.
Except the sketch she'd had drawn of him. Proof in her mind, this face, this man it belonged to, was the one who'd violated her eight years ago.
"Shona," Earle called.
She ignored him. Shoulder barged a bloke with beefy arms.
"Watch it."
"Sorry," she muttered.
The crowd was thickening. People swarming and bobbing up and down to the music. She lost sight of her target. Strained to see him again.
"There you are, you bastard." She spotted him, scooted forward, slipped around two fellas with girls balancing on their shoulders.
But in an instant, she'd lost him again. He'd melted into the crowd. Gone.
"No!" She broke into a run.
"Shona!" Earle was behind her.
She pushed past a group huddled together, sharing a bottle of vodka as they air punched to the beat.
Frustration burned in her veins. How could he have just vanished?
"Where are you going?" Earle said, his big fingers curling around her shoulder.
"Fuck." She spun a full circle.
"What?" he asked again.
"I saw someone."
"Okay...who?"
"Someone I know is a bad egg."
He raised his eyebrows. "Someone from when you used to live here? Years ago?"

"Yes." She was studying faces, scanning features. Eliminating everyone she rested her attention on. "He's up to no good if he's here. I know it."

"Perhaps he's changed. Turned over a new leaf."

She huffed. "Shit. I just saw him."

"Description." Earle looked over the heads of most people.

"Asian descent, gap in his teeth, monobrow. He had on a red t-shirt."

"Monobrow?"

"Yes, you know." She drew a line between her eyebrows with her finger. "No space here."

"Ah, got you." He squinted to the west then turned the other way, seeming to study the crowd.

"See him?" Shona asked, tapping her fingertips together.

"No, but it's kind of hard in a crowd. You must have a good memory. He'd have aged. Did you go to school with him?"

"No. And to be honest, he doesn't appear much different. Still an ugly bastard."

"Whoa, you really don't like him."

"I more than dislike him, he's a scumbag." She slammed her hands on her hips. "Fuck."

"Hey, chill out."

She pressed her lips together and closed her eyes. If there was one thing Shona hated it was being told to chill out. But she was behaving weird enough in front of Earle, without giving him a taste of her sharp tongue, too.

"If he wasn't doing anything wrong, you couldn't have brought him in anyway. Having a monobrow is hardly a crime."

She huffed and opened her eyes, resisted stomping her foot on the ground.

"Let's go. It's been a long day. You need to eat, and maybe use up that adrenaline in the gym."

Shona sighed, trying to release some of the tension that was coiled in her chest, seeming to squeeze her heart. "Yeah. You're right. Come on."

Shona drove to the dojo, but when she pulled up and spotted the time, she groaned. It was hardly worth getting changed into her gi. The training session she'd promised Ben she'd attend was almost over.

Gripping the steering wheel, she hung her head, let her hair fall forward, and closed her eyes. Seeing her attacker after all this time had been shocking, but far from wanting to shrink away from him, hide, she wanted to kick his arse, make him pay, get justice.

Yet just like that, water through her fingers, he'd disappeared. It was as if he'd magically been transported out of the festival.

But who was that he'd been talking to? Was it one of his accomplices of old? Partner in crime?

She thought back. He was tall, slim, his hair was light. Was it the creep who'd attacked Tina? She tried to recall. When under hypnosis, she'd seen him as weak-chinned, large protruding ears, but now, she couldn't remember what she'd seen at the festival. She'd been so focused on the Asian, her brain just hadn't processed anything about the man he'd been with.

She slammed her hands on the steering wheel. "Fuck it!"

Knock. Knock.

She jumped, sat upright, and pushed her hair over her shoulders.

Ben stood by her car door. His jawline was coated in dark stubble, and he wore a worried expression.

She wound down the window. "Hi."

"You okay?"

"Frustrating day at work."

"Ah. Sorry about that."

"Not your fault, Ben."

"I can still feel sorry about it."

She nodded at the entrance to KICKERS. "Apologies, I've missed the session. Busy, what with the festival and all that."

"I'm sure." He smiled. "But join us for dinner. We're going round the corner, to The Bay Leaf."

"I don't know, I should probably just go home."

"You have to eat, right?"

Her stomach clenched. She really was hungry. It was a long time since her cheese salad sandwich.

"It's nothing fancy but the food is always hot and fresh. Personally, I can't resist the madras."

"You like it hot, eh."

He laughed. "Hotter the better."

Shona found her door being opened.

He held out his hand. "Come on, no strings, just food with some new friends."

"I suppose I could do with both, the food and the friends." She smiled and stepped out. Shut the door. "Thanks, Ben. I appreciate it."

He tugged at his black North Face t-shirt, straightening a few creases, and beamed. "Some of the others will already be there."

"Okay." She locked her car, and they walked around the corner, past a chippy and a dry cleaners. "When is your sister back from her honeymoon?"

"Another week. They're spending some time in Sri Lanka after the Maldives."

"Sounds divine."

"Do you like to travel?"

"Yes, not that I have much. I've been too busy."

"Career been all consuming, eh?"

"Yes, focus, you know. I had my eye on what I wanted, worked for it. Got it."

"I admire that, very much."

Shona didn't say anything.

"Strength, energy, focus, great qualities," he went on.

"Karate helped with all of that."

"They had to be there to begin with. Karate nurtured them to full potential, that's all."

"I like that." She smiled and studied a hanging basket filled with scarlet fuchsia. She was glad she'd decided to go out for dinner with Ben and her new karate friends. It was a normal thing to do. A young woman type of evening, rather than brooding about revenge, sweating in the dojo after a twelve-hour day, or watching the soaps with her parents.

He set his palm in the dip of her back. "Here we are. The Bay Leaf. I hope you like it."

Ben opened the door, and Shona stepped inside the small, warm restaurant. It was half full. Several waiters dressed in smart black trousers and white shirts busied around. She breathed deep, inhaling the rich, fragrant scents.

But before the smell had truly hit the base of her lungs, she froze. The heady blend of spices, the thickness of the air, it was familiar.

Horribly familiar.

It took her back to when she'd been hypnotised.

Meredith leading her mind into a dark, scary past.

A past she didn't want to remember but had to.

The smell. Of her attacker. It was this. An exotic blend of spices laced with a slightly greasy thickness she hadn't been able to identify.

Until now.

It hadn't been his cologne she'd smelt when regressed to that fateful night. It was the air around them, around her, him, Nicola and Tina, too. They'd been near Indian cooking of some sort. No wonder sniffing the aftershaves at Frasers hadn't been fruitful, she'd been barking up the wrong tree. It was a food smell.

His face flashed before her. He was sneering and his eyes dark with menace.

She blew out a breath and beat down a full body tremble.

"You okay?" Ben asked, gently touching her forearm.

"Er...yes." She nibbled on her bottom lip. Studied every face in the room in one quick glance the way she was trained to do.

He wasn't there.

And why would he be?

There were several Indian restaurants in Ironash, plus takaways and plenty of people cooked food that smelt like this. Talk about needle and haystack.

But still, that didn't stop the hairs on the back of her neck tingling and her heart rate picking up. The smell was strong and real. A week ago she wouldn't have reacted but after hypnosis she had no choice but to acknowledge the emotions rushing through her.

And his face. Flashing in front of her like that. Fresh after witnessing it at the festival.

"They're over there." Ben pointed at a corner table. "Shall we?"

She swallowed. "I...yes. Okay."

"You've gone pale." Ben frowned. "You sure you're all right?"

She tipped her chin and forced a grin. "Just hungry, I suppose."

Stepping past him, she took a seat, smiling at the others at the table. She'd met them all on her previous visit to the dojo.

Ben sat next to her and handed her a menu. "Why don't you get a starter? The sooner you get food inside you the better."

Her first instinct was to say something about being able to decide for herself, but she held back. Ben was nice. More than nice. He was kind, thoughtful, and handsome. Her mother would tell her to enjoy being cared for. "I will, thanks."

He poured her a glass of water, then pulled a pair of small black glasses from his pocket and studied the menu.

Shona scanned the food options and tried to ignore the smell lacing the sides of her nostrils, her tongue, and her throat. It was seeping into her hair and clothes, seeming to become part of her skin and blood.

And she had to admit, it was part of her.

Chapter Nine

Olga stared at the tent Spencer had disappeared into. He was clearly drunk or high, maybe both, and she guessed he'd passed out.

But where were the others?

Again she looked around. The only thing she could presume was they all loved this shitty band and couldn't bear to miss out. Actually yeah, she recognised some of the corny lyrics. It was a popular song at the moment. Not her cup of tea, not by a long shot, but right now she was glad it was thundering from the stage. It gave her the advantage of surprise and one-on-one.

She sneaked forward, half stooped, her shadow stretching over four folding chairs set around a camping table littered with empty bottles of Prosecco, beer, vodka, and a Marlboro Lights packet.

Stupid Spencer. He really has been caning it all afternoon.

Her stomach did a flip of excitement and, clutching the knife still in her sleeve, she stooped and flicked open the entrance to the tent.

The light was dim, but Spencer was easily visible. Sprawled out on his back, mouth parted as he snored. With his arms at his sides, palms up, he was almost sacrificial.

How convenient.

After one last check over her shoulder, Olga ducked into the small two-berth tent. She crawled onto the airbed next to the one Spencer was prostrate on. Was this for Charles or Nancy? She'd put money on the latter. Slut. Wanker.

Carefully, she drew down the zip, stopping halfway during a lull in beating drums, but then carrying on when the crowd roared.

And then there she was. Alone. With Spencer Cambridge. The dickhead who'd ruined her life with his lies, his Judas' kisses, and empty promises. It had all meant nothing to him. *She* meant nothing to him.

Well. She'd show him what happened when he treated people like dirt—people who were stronger than they appeared. Who sought vengeance and would not allow humiliation to grind them down.

She tucked her hair behind her ears. Stroked her tongue piercing over the roof of her mouth, then pulled the bangle of duct tape from her right wrist.

Spencer released a long, groaning snore.

She froze.

His breathing continued, slow and deep.

He seemed really out of it. But would he wake if she touched him? Oh, she wanted him to, eventually. She wanted him to be awake for the horrors she had in store. Where would be the fun if he wasn't? How would he understand what he'd done had been wrong, so very wrong?

But she didn't want him awake yet. So she found the end of the tape, scratching at it with her black-varnished nail. If she didn't bite them it would be easier. But she did, always had. Nail biter, that was what she was.

She found the end, and quietly unpeeled it.

Spencer's ankles were on show, his socks having slipped down to his trainers and his jeans rucked up. Being as gentle as she could, Olga wrapped the duct tape around his lower legs, strapping them together. It stuck to his golden leg hairs. Not that it mattered.

Happy his legs were harnessed, she slowly rested first his right hand then his left on his abdomen. She watched his face all the time, checking for any changes in his features, in his breathing. There were none.

Once again she set to work, carefully wrapping duct tape around his wrists, binding them tightly together.

His skin was warm, his fingers elegant, like a pianist's. Her mind was full of memories of him touching her as though he liked her, wanted her. His flesh hot on hers, his breath breezing over her ear, the taste of his tongue on hers.

Desire warred with anger. If he hadn't made her long for him, for his caresses and kisses, this wouldn't be happening.

He only had himself to blame.

He inhaled deeply, grunted, kept the air in there, his chest swollen against his t-shirt, nipples just visible through the material.

Olga stared wide-eyed, perfectly still.

Still he didn't exhale. Each passing second without an expulsion of air had Olga's heart rate picking up. What if he died, like this? Before she taught him his lesson?

That wouldn't do at all.

And then he huffed out a long breath, muttering something with it. His chest deflated, his lips parted.

And then his steady, deep breathing continued. In and out. In and out.

Olga tore off an eight-inch strip of duct tape and hovered it over his face. This would be the moment he did wake up, she was sure of it. But for a few seconds she savoured looking at him, staring at his sprinkle of pale stubble, the perfect bow on his top lip, his freckles, his lashes, slightly curled and delicate.

He was almost pretty. Certainly prettier than she was.

But she knew a person could be attractive, handsome on the outside, but pure evil on the inside. Rotten to the core. That was what Spencer was. His face, body, his taste, and his smell had all been a trick to lure her in.

Now it was time for her trick.

She pressed the tape down over his mouth. Thick and wide and dark, it stuck fast to his skin.

He stirred, shifting his head from left to right. A snorting snore caught in his nose.

Olga took the knife from her sleeve. Holding it up, she made sure it was in his line of sight.

He opened his eyes. His lids heavy.

For a heartbeat he was still, unfocused, then his attention settled on the glinting blade. His eyes widened, his pupils dilated.

"Mmphf." He twitched, jerked his hands, then his legs. He twisted his torso, as if to roll over.

"Shh, keep still, Spencer." Quickly, she lowered the knife to his neck, lightly pressing it to where she imagined his carotid to be. It would be bigger than a mouse's main neck artery, much bigger. Curiosity nudged her. The need to know.

He froze. His Adam's apple dipped as he swallowed. The round lump almost scraped over the surface of the knife. It really wasn't sensible of him.

"Surprised to see me?" she asked, swiping her tongue over her lips.

A strangled sound gurgled from his mouth and was trapped by the duct tape covering his lips.

She tipped her head. "You've been drinking all afternoon, goodness knows what else you've taken." She paused, slid the knife over his skin, watching a faint red line bloom. "Got yourself really pissed up, didn't you."

"Mmm." A high-pitched, pathetic noise, accompanied by a flash of terror in his eyes.

"But this isn't a drunken dream, Spencer, oh no, this is real." She paused, glanced down his tightly tied body. "You really are gagged and bound and at my mercy."

He made more strange noises behind the tape. Each one reminded her of the wailing sobs she'd buried into her pillow after the photographs went live online, humiliation and shame tormenting her in sharp, relentless whips through her psyche.

"Doesn't feel great, does it, to be at someone else's mercy." She slid the knife back again, creating another thin blushed line.

He trembled. A full body shiver.

A lock of hair fell over his brow, the tip brushing his eye.

She stroked it away, the strand soft on her fingertips and his skin warm. "You thought it great Saturday night entertainment to trick me, didn't you, Spencer. Something to do because you were bored, is that right? Or did you just have a need to ruin someone's life? Because that's what you did. You ruined me. You made me feel less than an amoeba. You turned me into a laughing stock. Until you all came along, I kept to myself, stayed beneath the radar. I know I'm weird, I can't help that. But I didn't bother anyone, I'd never *hurt* anyone." As she'd said the word 'hurt', she'd slipped the sharp tip of the blade to the hollow of his throat and poked it until it made a deep dent. "Until now."

He was barely blinking, barely breathing. But she wasn't fooled by his stillness. Mr Kent had told them all about adrenaline and its effect on the body. And right now, despite having a high alcohol content, Spencer's blood would be pumped full of fight or flight.

"Until now," she repeated. "Because now I have this need for revenge. It's like a real living part of me. A monster that's craving vengeance. It's rattling the cage, begging to be set free, to run wild, rampage...to see blood." She drew the knife lower, the tip scraping at his t-shirt. She upended it over his heart. "*Your* blood."

"Mmm... Mmm..." He flinched.

"Keep still." She applied pressure to the blade.

He quietened. His cheeks were pale; the flush of booze had drained away.

"And this monster, he's a real bastard. He's demanding, loud, you know, in my head. He won't shut up, he won't be calmed." With her free hand she undid his belt. It was posh black leather, the buckle shiny gold. Once released, she let it hang free, like a snake dangling from his waist.

"Don't move, will you, Spencer. This knife is very sharp, as sharp as the comments under each picture you and your cronies posted. And that last post, of me on my knees, knelt before you with your dick..." She paused. Swallowed. "And your face was blurred out. You were too embarrassed to be seen getting a blow job from the Goth-fuck-freak, weren't you?"

Again he made a noise. This time he raised his hands, too.

"Ah, ah, no moving." She jabbed the knife harder, knowing the tip would have breached his skin. "We still have matters to address."

He dropped his hands to his belly and lay there, all of his brawn subdued by a few twists of duct tape and a knife at his heart.

Olga studied his eyes. Once, she'd stared into them with hope springing. Believing that she'd finally found someone to see the real her. Who saw beyond her crazy, unpredictable home life, her love of darkness, fascination with death and the occult. But his eyes had lied the same way his tongue had. Spencer hadn't seen her any more than any of the other idiots at college did. He'd labelled her a creepy freak in his mind, and that would never change.

So she may as well act like one.

"You thought it was fun to make me a laughing stock," she said, speaking a little louder now as the band picked up volume. "To reel me in with your lies and promises. Have you any idea how horrendous that was? How stupid I felt?"

He shook his head.

"Well, I'll tell you." She released the button on his jeans. "It made me feel small, insignificant, stupid, embarrassed." She drew down his flies.

"Mmm." His fingers splayed, he yanked at the tape.

"No! Keep still." She leaned right over him, her nose almost touching his. "Or I will kill you, Spencer. I'm only a second away from doing it anyway. One push of this knife, and it's all over."

He was unblinking. A small tremor shook his entire body. She'd love to know what was going on in his mind, but that would mean removing the tape from his mouth, and she didn't want to do that...not yet.

She sat back up, a rush of power filling her. It was a pleasant sensation, one she wanted more of. After having it bled from her that dreadful night, she'd been running on empty. And God, the knife she held at his heart. One push, one small jab of her hand, a flex of muscles in her arm, and it would be through his chest wall, slicing his ventricles and atrium. How easy it would be.

There was a noise outside, footsteps, a twang as a guide rope was tugged.

"Fuck," someone muttered.

Olga held her finger to her lips and glared at Spencer.

He stared back at her.

The passerby continued on their way.

"Good, they've gone. Now where were we?" Olga said, spinning the knife, so the blade screwed up his t-shirt. She spun it back the other way. "Ah yes, your dick."

"Mmmfph. Mmm."

She grinned, gleeful that he'd clocked on to her plan.

"You made me think you had feelings for me, in your heart and body." She reached into his underwear, pulled him out. It was soft, and she nipped the loose skin at the end, stretching it long and thin.

Olga didn't want to touch him, not really, but this was a means to an end.

He squirmed, breathing hard now, snorting, his chest expanding against the knife. Panic had really set in.

They were getting to the good bit.

"Do you feel scared? Humiliated? Anxious?" She paused. "Welcome to my world, Spencer."

Her heart was pounding, her skin hot. A flood of endorphins rushed through her. Revenge felt even better than she'd thought it would. She hadn't counted on the physical thrill of it.

"And now," she said. "To make sure you never deceive anyone again with your face, your words…your body."

Quick as a flash, she removed the knife from where it was perched over his heart and sliced it through the base of his dick. It wasn't a clean cut, the flesh was tendon rich, so it took a bit of sawing. Even so, it didn't take more than a couple of seconds.

He screamed against the tape.

Blood spurted, instantly filling his groin area, soaking his jeans.

"Shut up," she snarled, holding up the limp, amputated penis. "Shut the fuck up."

He arched his back, writhed. His eyes were screwed up tight. He kicked, rocked to the left and the right. Still the blood came.

She glanced at the door; the zip was still down tight. Soon she'd have to get out of there. Luckily, she was nearly finished.

"Be quiet." She set the knife over the top of his thigh, exactly where Mr Kent had said the femoral artery was.

Spencer continued to flail like a tortured animal.

Which she really couldn't be doing with.

She stabbed his upper leg and was rewarded with a gush of bright-red blood.

He won't last long now.

"Now you know how it feels to be worthless," she said, bending over him once more. "To be thrown to one side, discarded as if no one cares." She peeled back the tape covering his mouth.

His lips parted, ready to scream, even though he was weakening as his blood drained.

In one swift move, she shoved his cock into his mouth—fitting end after the pictures he'd posted of her—and slapped the tape back into place.

His cheeks bulged. Tears ran from his eyes, tracking sideways, towards his temples.

Olga smiled. "Goodbye, Spencer. What we had was fun while it lasted. But some love affairs are never meant to be."

The metallic scent of blood was strong now, filling the warm air. It was everywhere, too—on Olga's hands, her skirt, her top. Spencer was soaked in the stuff; his own life force had rushed from him as if wanting to be free.

For a moment she watched while he sagged, the fight leaving him. His eyes closed, his head fell to the right. His chest was barely moving.

He's nearly dead.

She wiped the blade on her skirt then hid it inside her sleeve again. As the band played its chorus, Spencer took his final breath.

Good.

One down. Three to go.

Chapter Ten

Shona opted for onion bhajis and then chicken korma. She'd had a few sips of wine then stuck to the iced water, knowing she was driving home.

The KICKERS karate gang were good fun. A lively lot with witty banter and clearly comfortable together. She thought she recognised one of the girls from school, but Shona had been younger than her, and with no reciprocal recognition, she kept quiet about it. These days she preferred to garner information rather than give it out.

After the bill had been split eight ways, people began to wander off.

"I'll walk you to your car," Ben said.

"I'll be fine." She stood.

"I know you will be, I've sparred with you, remember." He laughed and pushed his chair in. "But I'm an old-fashioned kind of guy. Women shouldn't be wandering the streets alone."

"If it makes you feel better, thank you."

"It will. And besides, my father would turn in his grave if I didn't."

"I'm sorry, that you lost your dad."

"It was a long time ago, and it wasn't your fault."

She smiled and inclined her head. She pointed at the sign for the toilet. "I won't be a moment."

"I'll wait outside."

She made her way around a couple of tables and a coatstand, then stepped back as a waiter rushed past holding a tray of pints. It was certainly a busy and popular place.

After pushing through a door painted scarlet, she found herself in a small corridor. The green lino was faded, and a big picture of an elephant adorned with intricate patterns listed to the left on the wall opposite.

In the confined space, the smell she'd been trying to ignore was even stronger. But she needed to go. It was a twenty-minute drive home if she got caught at every light.

Walking past a door leading to the gents, she found herself turning a corner. The restaurant had clearly been a house once upon a time, and a pink carpeted staircase led upwards beside the ladies'.

Shona stilled and stared up at it. Beneath a small window was a table draped in shiny red material. Sitting atop the table was a statue.

A Buddha.

Tightly coiled hair, eyes half closed, one hand raised, palm facing forward. A single marigold flower sat beside it.

She clasped her hand over her mouth, swallowed. The korma rolled over in her stomach. The last time she'd thought about a statue of Buddha she'd been hypnotised. It had come to her, loomed out of the dense, disorientating fog. The serene face and the meditative gaze had been a clear, intense image.

She glanced left and right.

She was alone.

The cogs of her mind turned. After years of being clueless, helpless, it was as if a jigsaw was slotting into place. She wasn't sure of the finished picture, or if she could finish it—some pieces were still missing.

But she was getting there, and this Buddha, the scents of Indian cooking. It was filling in empty gaps.

Her phone rang.

Still frowning at Buddha, she pressed it to her ear. "Hey, Earle. What's up?"

"I hope you haven't just settled down in your pyjamas with a hot chocolate."

"Nope, at an Indian restaurant actually, why?"

"We've got a body."

"What?" She spun around and strode back the way she'd come, hand outstretched ready to shove at the door.

"At the festival."

"Shit. I'm on my way." She burst into the gaggle of conversation filling the restaurant.

"See you there."

"At Central Control?"

"Yeah, they're keeping it on a need-to-know basis until the details are understood. Last thing we need is a bunch of hysterical, pissed festivalgoers."

"Got you."

She strode through the restaurant. Damn, she'd forgotten to go for a wee. That would have to wait now.

Pushing outside, she paced towards Ben, and then past him.

"Hey," he said, hurrying to keep up with her. "What's the rush?"

She threw him a frown accompanied with a sigh. "Something's come up."

"A life-or-death emergency, judging by your speed."

She kept walking. "I can't say. I have to go, sorry." Was it a suspicious death? Earle hadn't given her any information. It must be. Why else would they be there? And why hadn't Sergeant Nicols called her as she'd told her to?

"Shit, I'm sorry. It probably is death, isn't it?"

She sensed Ben coming to a halt behind her. She stopped, too, and turned. "I had a nice time, thank you for inviting me."

"You're one of the gang now, no thanks necessary." He grinned.

He had such a kind face and genuine smile that Shona regretted having to rush off. "Well, I appreciate it. I need something other than work, it's…"

"All-consuming."

"That's the word." She found her car keys. "Next training session is Monday, right?"

"Officially, yes, though if you ever want to help out with the junior grades they're in on a Saturday and Sunday morning."

"I'd like that." She smiled and nodded in the direction of her car. "Again, I'm sorry—"

"No apologies, you've got an important job to do. I hope it's nothing too serious."

"I fear it's about as serious as it gets."

Within thirty minutes, Shona was pulling back into the staff car park at the festival. The SOCO team had just arrived.

"Hey, Julie." Shona nodded.

Julie frowned through the fading light. "DI Williams. Wish I could say it was nice to see you, but it's never a good sign when our paths meet."

"Tell me about it."

Julie's team were whizzing around, gathering equipment and bags.

Earle appeared at Shona's side. "Sorry to interrupt your curry."

"I'd finished." Shona gestured to the control tent. "How come you got the call and not me? I asked…what's her name again?"

"Nicols, and she said she'd tried but it went straight to voicemail."

"What?" Shona retrieved her phone. Sure enough, there was a voicemail message. "Damn, it was loud in the restaurant, but I didn't think I'd miss a call." It was unlike her to be un-contactable. Perhaps it just proved she'd been having a nice time—that in itself was a novelty.

Earle shrugged. "No harm done, we're here now."

"Sounds like there's been harm done to someone."

Julie nodded up the hill. "The body is in a tent. We'll head there now."

"You suiting up?" Earle asked.

Julie looked at Shona. "If it's okay, we'll do that when we're at the site, save adding to the drama."

"I'm happy with that." Shona glanced towards the stage area. Lights danced into the sky. The crowd was dense, and beating music blasted out. "What time does this finish?"

"Whenever you want it to." Sergeant Nicols stepped up. "Just say the word, ma'am."

Shona nibbled on her bottom lip and turned to Earle. "I think it's okay to continue for now, until we know more about cause of death. And then I'll need to give Fletcher a call."

"I agree."

"Understood." Nicols pointed at the spread of tents to the right. "I'll show you the way."

They stomped after her, walking past small dwindling bonfires, tents that had been decorated with bunting and flags, couples sitting entwined, and tables laden with cans and the remnants of barbecue suppers.

"It's growing every year, this sea of tents," Earle said.

"Which just increases the chance of incidents." Shona studied the woodland stretching over the horizon. It was dark, creepy, and she couldn't help but wonder what lurked there—or who lurked there.

"It's over here." Nicols marched to the right.

The SOCO team followed, along with a crime scene photographer.

Several uniforms were standing, feet apart, arms crossed, surrounding a tent. Luckily, there were no spectators. Seemed the band currently playing had taken everyone's attention.

Nicols pointed at a tall officer with dark hair. "The male body was discovered by a young female, Nancy Braithwaite, eighteen, who then found Sergeant Frost."

"His girlfriend?" Shona asked.

"I haven't got that far. She's somewhat hysterical. Keeps asking for Charles and Rebecca. We haven't located them yet."

"Where is she? Nancy?"

"With a female officer, down at the control tent."

"Okay. We'll speak to her later."

The SOCO team suited up in the dim light. Torches were flashed, and blue tape was strung out to cordon off the scene.

"This won't be a secret for long." Shona signed the log before putting on a white overall, boots, and gloves.

"Yeah, word will spread quickly." Earle copied Shona. "Got a plan?"

"We'll cross that bridge when we come to it. This is a big crowd who've paid a lot of money to be here."

"Yeah, never know, might be natural causes."

Shona raised her eyebrows at him.

"A bloke can hope." He shrugged.

Julie, now also dressed in a white suit, pulled back the opening to the tent. They all crouched to peer inside. The photographer clicked away.

"Oh shit." Shona sucked in a breath and grimaced. Just when she thought she'd seen everything, here was a new degrading, sick way to be killed.

"Definitely not natural causes," Earle mumbled.

The young man flat on his back before her had his wrists and ankles wrapped in dark-grey duct tape. His blood-soaked jeans were undone and shoved down, creases angled around his groin. But his groin...

That was one hell of a mess. A stump was all that remained of his penis and his pubic hair was heavily matted with congealed blood.

"Gordon Bennett," Julie muttered. "This is a blood bath." She was right, the red stuff was everywhere. On the walls of the tent, the floor, and all over the body. "I'd say he's had a femoral artery punctured as well as penile. Coroner will say for sure when he's cleaned up and taken a closer look, but it's a safe bet."

"Would have been quick then," Shona muttered. "Damn waste of a young life."

Earle tutted and released a frustrated sigh.

"You okay for me to go in?" Julie asked.

"Rather you than me." Shona nodded.

Carefully, Julie made her way alongside the body. She reached for the tape over the victim's mouth. "I'm going to remove this."

"Go ahead." Shona wished the music would stop, it was giving her a headache.

Slowly, Julie peeled back the tape. The pale lips were stained with blood, and it was clear the mouth wasn't completely shut.

"What the hell is in there?" Earle asked.

Shona swallowed. Surely it wasn't what she thought it was.

"Removing lodged object." Julie carefully gripped the bloody end of whatever was stuffed in the corpse's mouth. She pulled, slowly.

What appeared to be a bloody sausage was revealed.

"I think this used to belong to a different part of his body," Julie said, holding it up in the torchlight.

A photograph was snapped.

Earle groaned. "Jesus Christ."

"Someone really did a number on him." Shona nodded at the penis. "What do you think amputated it?"

Julie studied the end. "I'd say a knife. Not surgical sharpness but pretty sharp, and a good size, too. Carving perhaps."

"This is making me want to vomit." Earle swallowed loudly.

"Don't look anymore." Shona rested her hand on his upper arm. "We can assume its murder. We'll let SOCO do their stuff now."

Earle stood and stepped away. He pressed his hands to his waist, tipped his head to the sky, and blew out a breath.

"Doesn't matter how big and tough they are," Julie said, "the thought of their dick, or anyone's dick getting hacked off, makes them want to puke."

"Can't blame him." Shona studied the body. "He didn't fight back from what I can tell."

"No, there doesn't appear to have been a struggle."

"Drunk?" Shona wondered. "Knife held to his throat? Seems to be marks there."

"Yeah, a big, threatening attacker, who easily subdued him?"

"I suppose. Do we have a name?"

"The girl, Nancy, gave it as Spencer Cambridge. He's a twin apparently."

"The twin is here, at the festival?"

"I'm guessing it's the Charles that Nicols mentioned. You could ask the officer outside, Frost I think his name is."

"Okay, stay in touch with anything you find."

"Will do."

Shona stood, her knees a little damp from kneeling. "You spoke to the girl who found the body?" she asked the officer she'd first seen when she'd arrived at the scene.

"Yes, ma'am."

"And the victim, Spencer Cambridge, is a twin. Is the twin here?"

"I believe his name is Charles. Nancy asked us to find him, and a Rebecca Smith-Brown."

"Are you doing that?"

"We're on the case." Nicols stepped up. "Not easy, though, especially now it's dark."

"Needs to be done. See if you can get a photo of them, from this Nancy. Give it to the security blokes, too. I want them found ASAP."

Shona had a bad feeling. Despite the party atmosphere, the maze of tents, black sky, and shadowy people meant it was just a nudge away from chaos—the perfect place for attackers to seek out victims.

Chapter Eleven

Olga kept her head bowed as she rushed past the straw bales and back to her tent. Her long black skirt was weighted with Spencer's blood, and her hands, stained bright red—but curled up in her sleeves, the left holding the knife— couldn't be seen, and in the darkness her skirt absorbed the blots and smears, making them invisible to anyone who might have glanced her way.

She removed her boots outside her tent, then ducked in. She set the knife to one side—the blade and handle were smeared with darkening blood.

Quickly, she stripped down to her underwear and shoved her clothes into one of the black bin liners she'd brought. When she got a chance, back at home, she'd burn the evidence.

Using baby wipes, bought especially for the job, she set about scrubbing Spencer from her hands and face. Her thighs were also mottled with his blood, some of it having seeped through the material of her skirt. The pile of now pink wipes grew, the powdery smell a welcome relief after the tang of blood.

Soon she was dressed again. This time in black jeans, a rip on the right knee—not intentional, but luckily it passed as fashion. She glanced in a small pocket mirror, tutted at a streak of red over her right cheek. She grabbed another baby wipe, destroyed that bit of evidence. Then quickly, she added powder to her face, another layer of black eye liner, and a swipe of dark-purple lipstick.

She thought back to how Spencer's mouth had looked when it was stuffed full of his cock.

Not so bloody easy to lie now is it, prick?

She chuckled. Killing him had been easier than she'd thought it would be, more fun, too. She hadn't anticipated the sense of power, or the fear in his eyes. Both had been added extras. It seemed being in control was pretty cool. Something she should experience more of.

She reached for the Charles doll. He'd be next. Carefully, she set his cut-off hands on his belly. His fate couldn't be changed, not now. His path was set.

But she couldn't sit around all night listening to that god-awful music and playing voodoo, she had work to do. So after munching a Crunchie bar and taking a swig of warm cola, she headed out again, knife once more hidden in her sleeve, the dirty blade against her arm. She'd left the blood on it, kind of a souvenir. It would be easy enough to clean if she had to. On her opposite wrist she wore her duct tape bangle.

She grabbed a torch and shoved it in her back pocket, pulled the zip on her door, and took in the field of tents to her right. There seemed to be some extra movement in the area of Spencer's, but she couldn't be sure. He'd be found sooner or later…though later would serve her well.

Boots on and with her hair hanging limply around her cheeks, her fringe catching in her eyelashes, she walked around the straw bales.

But she stopped in her tracks when she spotted two figures heading her way. Hand in hand, the bloke was tall and broad-shouldered, the girl petite and in a pathetically tiny dress, her skinny legs poking from the hemline. She was lucky they held her upright.

Olga recognised them. Or at least she hoped she did.

Charles and Rebecca.

Was it, though?

And why were they heading in her direction? They didn't know she was at the festival. She certainly hadn't posted on Facebook about it the way they had been for weeks.

Quickly, she slipped around the side of the bales again, hiding from their line of view.

As they got closer, their voices drifted. Olga held her breath and pressed against the straw. Several strands poked at her shoulder and cheek.

"Why are we coming out here?"

Yes! It was Rebecca, that plummy voice was unmistakable.

"I told you, I wanted you to myself for a while."

Charles, too. Cocky. Confident. Complete arsehole.

"But I really like this band."

"So do I, but they'll play again tomorrow."

"Do you really think so?" Rebecca sounded doubtful.

"Yes."

Olga peeked around the bales. Rebecca and Charles were on the dark side now, facing the woods, hidden from most of the tents and the stage.

But not hidden from me.

"It's a bit cold," Rebecca said.

"Here, wear this." He removed a scarf, it had Bad Boys written on it, and placed it around her neck.

"Thanks." She smiled up at him.

He spread his arms and stepped forward, trapping Rebecca against the straw with his big body.

She looked up at him and giggled.

Olga hardly dared to breathe. She was so close to them. And were they about to…

She didn't know how she felt about watching them bump uglies. She'd be sick if she had to.

"Charles," Rebecca said, looping her hands around his neck. "We should get back to the stage. Nancy and Spencer will wonder where we are."

"Nancy won't notice, she was dancing like a loony last time I saw her, and Spencer is sleeping off his afternoon drinking."

"But—"

"If they do, they'll just presume we've gone off to make our own music." He kissed her, crushing up to her body in a nausea-inducing hip grind. "Don't worry about it, babe."

Olga blew her cheeks up and pressed her piercing to the roof of her mouth. She'd rather die than kiss Charles, or Spencer—not that he'd be kissing anyone ever again.

I wonder if he'll go to Hell. Probably.

Charles' hands wandered, slipping up the inside of Rebecca's dress.

"Hey," she said, shifting away. "Not now. Not that."

"But you promised. You said we would at the festival."

"Not out here."

"You said not in the tent either." He paused. "Have you changed your mind?"

"I still love you, Charles, but..."

"So you have." He stepped away. Lifted his hands then dropped them to his sides, his palms slapping on his jeans.

"It's just...I spoke to my mother."

"Fuck." He ran his hand through his hair. "Why would you do that?"

"Because we're close." She pushed away from the straw, reached for him. "We tell each other everything."

"You don't tell your mother you're going to fuck your boyfriend."

"It's more than fucking...you said it would be making love."

He pulled in a deep breath and blew it out slowly. "Of course it will be." His voice quieted to a deep, persuasive tone. "Come on, there's no one here, it won't take long."

"I'm not sure." She glanced in Olga's direction.

Olga whipped her head out of sight, crossed her fingers, and hoped to heck she hadn't been seen. After a moment, she peered cautiously around the bales again.

"Come on, I want you and I know you want me." He slipped his hands around her waist, kissed her forehead.

"I just don't think I'm ready. I mean, are we really serious, Charles?"

"Of course we are."

"But..."

"There's still a but?" He released her and stepped away, his shoulders tense and drawn up to his ears. "You said we would, Rebecca."

Olga had to keep herself from groaning. The whine in Charles' voice was pathetic. He was like a puppy being denied a treat.

"I'm sorry." Rebecca shrugged.

"You're sorry." He turned and pointed at the forest. "So I'm supposed to just go off and have a wank now, am I? Sort myself out."

"Charles."

"Well? Tell me. What am I supposed to do with this?" He pointed at his groin.

Rebecca raised her chin and folded her arms. "I'm sure you'll figure it out."

"Yeah, actually, I will." He cupped his groin. "And for the record, I won't be thinking about you, Rebecca, you're nothing but a prick tease. I'll be thinking about Clare Wright. I hear she does spread her legs."

"Charles!"

He stuck his middle finger up then spun around and paced towards the treeline.

Olga's legs twitched. She needed to follow him. Charles alone in the woods was a gift from Satan himself, proving she was doing the right thing by killing him and his dreadful twin.

"Knob!" Rebecca yelled, then broke into a run and raced around the opposite end of the straw bales and out of Olga's sight.

"Perfect." Olga smiled and started off after Charles.

With no moon and her black clothing, she wasn't too worried that he'd turn and see her. Here they were doused in darkness, and the woods would be darker still.

As she covered ground, having to go fast to keep up with Charles' long strides, the music faded. Olga's pulse thrummed in her ears, and her back became damp with sweat. She was excited, apprehensive, and a little fearful Charles might not be as easy to overpower as his drunken brother had been.

He climbed a fence and disappeared into the woods.

Olga broke into a run, also climbed the fence, then stood still and listened.

To her right, the crunch of leaves and a twig snapping.

She followed, using her ears as much as her eyes.

She, too, stood on a small branch. It cracked. She froze. Had he heard her?

It didn't seem so; his noisy footsteps didn't falter.

She rushed after him, thankful her eyes were adjusting to the dim lighting. She couldn't see clearly, but she could make out shapes. Soon she'd use her torch, but not yet. It wasn't time. It would give her away.

With her hand on the gnarled trunk of a tree, she paused. She was a little out of breath.

Charles was not far in front of her.

He'd stopped, too. She could make out his shoulders and his long torso highlighted by his neon-blue t-shirt—was it a football shirt?

"Fucking bitch," he muttered.

Olga had no intention of watching him relieve his sexual frustration, so deciding it was time to act, she drew the knife from her sleeve.

Moving forward, her boot knocked on a solid lump. A stone.

She smiled, an idea forming, and reached for it with her free hand. The stone was heavy and cool, and her fingers curled pleasingly around it. She took a step closer to Charles. He was about ten paces away.

"Prick tease," he grumbled. "Said she would. Bitch."

Olga raised the rock above her head, stared at the back of Charles'. Curiosity gnawed at her with each step. What would it feel like to bring it down on his skull? How much pressure would she need to knock him out?

She was so close now. A metre away. She held her breath. Lunged forward. Dropped her arm.

Whack!

The stone tumbled to the right. Charles tumbled to the left.

She stared, wide-eyed.

There'd been no staggering. No scream. Nothing. He'd hit the woodland floor like a sack of potatoes.

Quickly, she flicked the torch on and shone it at the back of his head. Blood was seeping onto his silky blond hair, and a curl of skin had peeled back from his scalp. She rushed over to him, examined his face. His eyes were closed, his lips slightly parted.

Have I killed him? Already?

That didn't sit well with her. She needed Charles to know why he was meeting his bad end. Understand exactly what he'd done wrong and who was taking revenge.

With the toe of her boot, she dug him in the ribs.

He groaned, and his features contorted.

Good. Not dead.

But she had to act fast.

Stooping, she set the knife and torch aside and slid the duct tape bangle from her wrist.

The same way she had with Spencer—it worked, why change a proven method?—she bound his ankles together. But instead of strapping his hands with the tape, Olga spread them wide, so he was on his back, arms out, crucifix pose.

Beside his left hand was a fallen tree trunk. A branch stuck towards them, hovering over his arm. It would do perfectly.

Olga set to work with the tape. She didn't care about the screechy, sticky noise. It would only take a moment.

She attached his left forearm, with copious amounts of tape, to the heavy trunk. That should immobilise him as much as she needed him to be.

She then tossed the roll of tape aside and balanced the torch on the trunk so it was shining on Charles. She wanted to witness every gory detail.

He moaned and shifted his head from left to right. The gash on his crown scraped through the leaves, dirt, and vegetation.

Thanking the good-luck demon for how this plan was going, she straddled his chest using her left knee to keep his right shoulder fastened securely to the ground.

He really was so similar to his murdered twin.

"Charles," she murmured, wielding the knife. "Oh, Charles, do wake up."

"Mmm..." He grunted and bared his gritted teeth as though becoming conscious of the pain in his scalp.

"Got a headache, have you?" She held the knife above his face so it would be the first thing he saw when he opened his eyes. "What a shame."

His eyelids raised, his pupils contracting in the white torchlight. "What...what the fuck!" He went to move but stilled when he focused on the knife. "Jesus, get the hell off me." He yanked his arm, his attention shifting from the blade to the tape binding him to the log. "Undo that...shit...who are you?" He stared up at her.

"Surely you remember? You took enough photographs of me."

"Olga Umbridge. Shit. You really are a sick, weird bitch. Undo me...now."

"I don't think you're in any position for name-calling or making demands, Charles." She turned the knife over, twice, enjoying the way the glinting light had him snatching in a breath.

"Please. Let me go."

"Begging, are you?"

"No, I'm asking."

There was a defiant twist to his lips that sent a new spurt of anger into Olga's bloodstream. How dare he think, in this position, that he had any control over the situation.

"And why should I do what you want me to?" She threw his words from *that* night back at him.

"You're still pissed off about that? Jesus, it was..."

"Don't say it was just for a laugh, because did you see me laughing?"

He yanked his left arm again, succeeding only in tightening the tape and rolling it into strong binds. The log didn't budge.

He kicked his legs, his knees banging her back. Rolled his hips as if trying to shake her off.

He shifted his right shoulder, raising his arm, and she increased her weight on that side to keep it pinned to the ground.

"Keep fucking still," she snarled, lowering the knife so it hovered over his right cheek.

"I'm sorry, okay. We're sorry."

"And what good does that do me?"

"I'll take the pictures down from Facebook, so will the others, I promise."

"Spencer won't."

"He will. I'll make him, Olga. We didn't mean any harm."

Good, there was fear in his voice now.

"Yes, you did. You wanted to humiliate me. You all did. I was your entertainment one Saturday night. I wasn't doing you any harm, keeping myself to myself, and yet you still decided I was your target."

He swallowed. His eyes were so wide all of the whites were visible.

"Spencer screamed when I taught him his lesson," she said. "But the tape over his mouth muffled the sounds."

"Spencer. What the hell have you done with Spencer?" There was a shake in his tone. The usual confident, cocky lilt had evaporated.

"What do you think I've done?" She turned the knife over again.

"I don't know."

"There's a clue on this knife. See this blood...it's your brother's."

"Shit. What? No." He was pale now. The colour rushing from his face. "Where is he? Does he need an ambulance?"

"Bit late for an ambulance."

"Jesus Christ, you're crazy."

"Yes, that's right." She tipped so close her face was only inches from his, the knife between them. "Crazy Olga, freaky Olga, weirdo Olga, what other names do you have?"

"None, I swear. Please let me go."

"No. It's too late for that." She looked at his right hand, twisted on the ground, dirt and leaves stuck to it. "It's time for you to pay for what you did to me."

With a long, sweeping movement, she brought the knife down on the crease of his wrist, slicing through flesh and tendon, arteries and veins until she hit bone.

He screamed, a high-pitched, panic-ridden yelp.

She ignored him. They wouldn't be heard here, not over the din of the music. And besides, it was quite nice to hear his pain.

She raised the knife, brought it down again, hard. It wasn't easy, though. His bones were strong and thick, a cleaver or axe would have served her better.

But she kept on going despite him bucking beneath her. She needed his hand off. That way he'd learn that using these vile fingers to operate a phone, take pictures without permission, wasn't something he should be doing.

His yells increased. He thrashed, fought the tape strapping his ankles and left arm. Olga was heavy, though, and had him well secured.

Finally, his hand came away from his wrist. Arcs of blood burst from the harshly cut, ragged stump, rushing to the forest floor, escaping his body.

"Now you know," she said, picking up his severed hand and dangling it over his face by the index finger. "What damage can be done when you post what you shouldn't. You should have thought about the consequences, Charles. You should have understood that when I said I'd kill you for it...I would."

His cries were quietening, his lips turning a strange mauve. He stopped kicking, stopped yanking at his left arm.

Olga sat up straight, her weight fully on his chest now. But his breaths were shallow, his ribs barely expanding. Again that flush of power spread over her skin like a caress. No longer the victim, she was now the architect of a plan, and boy did it feel good to be carrying it out. When she'd completed her task, she'd be on cloud nine.

Nothing could stop her.

Chapter Twelve

Shona and Earle removed their protective clothing then made their way to Central Control to speak to Nancy Braithwaite, pausing at the Portaloos on the way. When they arrived inside, she was sitting with a grey blanket over her shoulders and sipping from a plastic cup. Her blonde hair was messy, and what had been a yellow-and-pink flower painted on her cheek had smudged.

A female officer sat beside her. Neither of them were speaking.

"Hello," Shona said with a smile and brought up a chair. "Nancy, yes?"

The young woman nodded. Her hands were shaking and her red-rimmed eyes tear-filled.

"I'm sorry for your loss," Shona said, sitting then resting her hand on the girl's knee.

"It was such a shock, so much…blood." Nancy swallowed and downturned her mouth. "Poor, poor Spencer. Who would do such a thing? And his brother, Charles, he's going to be…oh, how must it feel to lose a twin, I…" Her voice trailed off, and she gulped down a sob.

"We really need to find Charles," Shona said. "He's here at the festival, right?"

"Yes."

"Where did you last see him?"

"By the stage, we were dancing to Bad Boys."

"Just the two of you?"

"No, his girlfriend, my best friend, Rebecca, too. She was with us."

"And then what happened?"

"I turned around, and they'd gone. I wasn't too worried. I guessed they'd gone back to the tents. Charles was…"

"What?"

"I doesn't matter." She looked down at the cup.

"It might matter. It might be very important."

She sighed. "Charles was pressurising Rebecca, you know to...do it."

"Okay."

"And I just thought that's why they'd gone from the stage area."

"Can you tell us what happened next?"

"I waited until the end of that song, but then I was thirsty. It's been a hot day, I was dancing and singing, you know, dries the throat."

Shona nodded.

"So I decided to go back to our tents. Spencer, he..." She paused, wiped at a tear trickling down her left cheek. "He..."

The female officer handed her a tissue.

"Thanks." Nancy pulled in a shaky breath. "Spencer had hit the beer all afternoon. I'd told him to drink some water with it, but he hadn't. So of course he was really drunk by the time the first act hit the stage. He said he felt sick, so I told him to go and lie down for an hour and then he'd be able to enjoy the rest of the music. He said he would, and that he'd find the tent okay on his own. So I let him go...but oh...I wish I hadn't, if only—"

"If onlys don't help," Shona said. "And to be honest, you could have become a victim, too."

Her eyes widened. "You think someone would have killed me?"

"It's a possibility." Shona glanced at Earle. This was a horrible case. These poor youngsters.

"Do you know anyone who might have wanted to hurt Spencer?" Earle asked, his pen poised over his notebook.

"No, he's popular, liked by everyone. Hell, most guys want to be him, and all the girls want to be *with* him. He's a great laugh, a good boyfriend...he *was* a good boyfriend. Oh dear..." She pressed her hand over her brow.

"Anyone he's had a falling out with recently?" Shona asked.

"Not that I can think of."

"Does he use social media?" Earle questioned.

"Yes, all the time. Facebook mainly. Encouraged others to stick with Facebook. Said he wanted to be the next Zuckerberg so it was all research for when he set up his own big thing."

"Okay, we'll investigate that." Shona turned to Earle. "I think it would be worth waking up Andy and seeing if he'll do some digging while this is still fresh."

"I'll get on it." Earle nodded.

"Oh, his mum and dad," Nancy wailed and set her cup aside, a slosh leaping over the rim. "They're in Austria, hill walking or something. This will crush them…"

"We'll get in touch with his parents," Shona said. "Don't worry about that. But back to Charles and Rebecca. They weren't in the tent next to Spencer, so where do you think they went?"

"I don't know. I really don't. I…"

"Nancy!" A young woman in a short flowery dress and with a long scarf around her neck rushed into the control tent.

A uniform stepped in behind her.

"Rebecca." Nancy jumped up, the blanket falling to the floor. A new wave of sobs choked from her chest.

"Oh God, what is happening?" Rebecca dragged Nancy into a hug.

"Spencer…he's…oh God, he's dead."

"Dead. But…?"

"Murdered." Nancy's face crumpled.

Rebecca stared around, disbelief flashing in her eyes. "They brought me here, said there'd been an incident and I was wanted for questioning. But Spencer, murdered, that can't be true."

"I'm afraid it is." Shona stood and guided the two girls into chairs. "Sit down, please."

They did as instructed, still clinging to each other.

"We need to find Charles Cambridge," Shona said, her attention on Rebecca. "Have you seen him recently?"

"Yes, about twenty minutes ago."

"And where was that?"

"Around the back of some hay bales, or straw bales, I don't know which. Why?"

"If someone set out to hurt his twin, perhaps they have Charles on their radar, too."

"Shit!" Rebecca slapped her hand over her mouth. "He went into the woods."

"The woods?" Nancy asked through her tears. "Why?"

"Well, he wanted to..." Rebecca shrugged. "And I said no." She looked at Shona. "We had a bit of an argument, he stormed off."

Shona's heart rate romped up, and a shiver crawled up her spine. This screamed of a disaster just waiting to happen.

"We need to find him, now." She stood and turned to Earle. "Get the uniforms out there searching. Start at the tree line and work into the forest."

Earle nodded.

"Dogs, too, as quickly as we can get them here." She glanced at the girls. "We need something belonging to Charles, for the scent."

"Here." Rebecca pulled the scarf from her neck. "This is his, he only bought it today, but he wore it all afternoon."

"Perfect." Shona set her attention on the female officer. "You got this?"

"Yes, ma'am."

Within thirty minutes, twenty uniforms were starting their search of the woods, and a van with two police search dogs had arrived.

"Andy," Shona said, answering her phone as she stared into the gloomy tree line. "Thanks for getting straight to this, especially with everything you've got going on." She pinched the bridge of her nose, remembering the recent death of his stepfather.

"No problem, I was awake anyway."

"Sorry again, for your loss."

"Thanks." He cleared his throat. "It's a pretty easy one, this case, on the face of it at least."

"Hold on a sec." She tapped her screen, setting it to speaker. "Earle is listening in, too."

"Gotcha. Okay, Spencer Cambridge, one thousand, two hundred and five friends on Facebook, mostly local from what I can see, though there's a cluster in Australia, not surprising as some of his photographs are showing a holiday out there last year, with his family. Seems like they were visiting relatives or something."

"What else?"

"He's in a bunch of public groups ranging from football-themed to movies and one secret group."

"Who's in the secret group?"

"Only five people."

"Hit me with them."

"Nancy Braithwaite, Rebecca Smith-Brown, his twin, Charles, and one other female, Olga Umbridge."

"Olga Umbridge. What have you got on her?"

"Well, at first glance, that's all I've had time to do so far, there's no mention in the group about her attending the festival, though the others have lots of posts about how they were looking forward to it and what they were bringing et cetera."

"So this Olga is part of their little gang, but not part of this event." Shona paused. "I'll ask Nancy and Rebecca about her."

"I'll keep digging, shall I? Go back a bit further."

"Yes, and if there's a picture of Olga Umbridge on her profile page, send that to me."

"There is."

"Great. Thanks again." She ended the call.

Within a few seconds her phone flashed, and she opened an image of Olga Umbridge. "What do you think?" She turned it Earle's way.

"Goth, huh."

"Mmm." Shona frowned. "Not the kind of girl I'd have expected this group to include."

"They didn't. She's not here."

"True. But do you think not being invited to join them at a music festival is enough to send her murderous?"

"And could she even carry it out?" Earle asked.

Shona zoomed in on Olga's face. "She's got sad eyes, what you can see of them through all that liner."

"It would be worth questioning her."

"I agree. I'll send Andy a message, find out her address, and we can do that tomorrow."

"Right now, tomorrow feels like a long time away." Earle sighed.

"You did eat, right, before you called me?"

"Yes, and luckily I'd just got the velvet cake out of the oven."

"Looking good?"

"Yep, smelt it, too."

She pressed her stomach. "Don't, you're making me hungry, and I shouldn't be, not after all that curry."

"Which Indian did you go to?"

"The Bay Leaf. Been there?"

"Once, ages ago with…"

"With?"

He paused. "Your predecessor. He liked a hot vindaloo washed down with a cold pint." There was something a little wistful in his voice, as though his mind had gone to another time and place.

Shona squeezed her lips together to hold in a tumble of questions. Now wasn't appropriate. Would it ever be?

Suddenly there was a racket from the trees. Dogs barking, several shouts. A uniform rushed out, waving his arms, the torch he was holding sending beams of light up into the sky.

"Shit." Shona broke into a run.

Earle was at her side, then a pace in front. "What is it?" he shouted as they neared.

"A body."

"What? Fuck!" The feeling of dread that had been sitting in Shona's stomach swelled, taking away any thoughts of red velvet cake. "Where?"

"A hundred yards in and to the east."

"Definitely dead?"

"Yep, afraid so."

"Shit, shit, shit," she muttered again. "And I know you're going to tell me it's a teenage male with blond hair, right?"

"Yes, ma'am. Sorry, ma'am."

She looked at Earle. "Julie's still at the first scene. Can you go and fill her in, ask her to come as soon as possible, and until then send some SOCOs to help secure the location."

"Will do." He turned and jogged back towards the tents.

"Lead the way," she said to the uniform.

After climbing a fence, the officer shone his torchlight at the woodland floor. It was dense with leaves and ferns and strewn with twigs, branches, and small round rocks.

"This is ancient and protected," he said. "Can't be built on."

"Good." Shona's mind wasn't on the trees, it was on the case. If Rebecca had seen Charles so recently, this was a fresh murder. The culprit couldn't be far. "I need the sweep of the woodland to continue, the perimeter watched, too. Whoever did this could be hiding in the cover of trees. We can flush them out."

"Of course, I'll see to that."

"Thanks."

"Not far now."

A huddle of officers, all with torches, came into sight. Shona rushed to the scene.

"I've started a log," one said, holding out his notebook.

"Good thinking." Shona signed in. "Where's the body?"

"Just over there, the other side of that fallen trunk. Only Sergeant Hill here has been into the area, he checked for a pulse." He handed her a powerful torch. "Sadly, there wasn't one."

"Thanks." She took the torch. "I'll wait until I get suited up before I approach." She walked to the reel of blue tape that had been hastily tied between trees and stood with one hand on her hip, the other shining her light at Charles Cambridge's hacked body.

Someone had really done a number on his right wrist. It was a bloody stump with tissue and tendons hanging from it, what appeared to be shards of bone, too. The hand itself was resting on his chest, fingers spread over his heart and looking weirdly like a caring touch. Blood had seeped from the end onto his bright-blue football shirt staining it dark.

"Who the hell did this to you?" she muttered, shaking her head. "Some right sicko."

He'd been tied by his left hand to a fallen tree trunk, with what appeared to be tape. Lots of it. It was tight, too, probably from where he'd struggled against it.

Duct tape? Also used on his twin...

Shona was in no doubt this hideous act was carried out by the same person—someone who really hadn't liked the brothers. Seemed they weren't as popular as Nancy thought they were.

She rubbed her chin. His ankles were also bound together with duct tape, and beneath his body the woodland debris had been disturbed and scattered. He'd put up a fight.

She thought again of the young Goth girl whose image sat on her phone. Could it really be a female killer? Both Charles and Spencer were strapping young men, likely fit, athletic, able to hold their own. Whoever did this had strength and cunning. A teenage girl with a grudge about missing out on festival fun—that just didn't add up.

It was then her attention fell on something. She shone the light on it. A roll of duct tape. Discarded and thrown to the right of the body, settled against a tree root.

"Hey, Sergeant Hill," she called. "Come here."

He was quickly at her side.

"Did you see that before?" She kept the beam on the tape.

He peered at it. "No, ma'am."

"I want it bagged, carefully, and checked for fingerprints as a priority. Make sure SOCO do it as their first job on arrival into the area."

"Yes, ma'am. Certainly, ma'am."

Chapter Thirteen

Olga had stumbled into her tent as several uniformed police officers had rushed past the straw bales. There were dogs as well, two of them. It wouldn't be long until Charles was found, and if they were looking for him, her suspicion that Spencer's body had also been discovered was right.

But that was okay, she was cracking on nicely with her plan. The two blokes, who she'd anticipated being the hardest to bump off, had offered themselves up like fresh meat.

She did up the zip on her tent and set about stripping off. She had a fresh black bin liner for these clothes and stuffed them in. They weren't as bloody as Spencer's had been, but she'd still burn them. It was worth losing half-decent jeans to destroy evidence.

The knife glinted up at her. It really was very bloodstained now, could probably do with sharpening, too. Charles' wrist had been pretty tough to get through once she'd hit bone.

But she'd done it, and hearing him wail in agony had been an added pleasure. The sounds had matched the agonies she'd experienced when the pictures of her naked, on her knees, had been posted online. Now he knew what it felt like to be tortured—though sadly, he wouldn't be able to reflect on it.

She used the baby wipes again and added them to the black bag of clothes. She dressed once more, this time in Lycra leggings that had gone bobbly between the thighs and the old Iron Maiden hoody. Normally she wouldn't be seen dead in Iron Maiden, but needs must, and this had only been hanging around at home.

With a giggle, she ran her hand over the letters on the front. Seen dead. What a good joke.

Rebecca's and Nancy's dolls stared up at her with their small, unblinking eyes.

"Who next?" She poked at their faces with her fingernail—pretty faces that hid evil souls.

Like Spencer and Charles, she supposed her next victim would be whichever one of the girls offered themselves up the most conveniently. It didn't really matter. She'd get them both in the end.

She picked up her phone and dialled the home landline. She'd promised to call her mother when it got dark so she wouldn't worry. There was no answer. Likely she was caught up with her balloons. Her latest colour was white, and she'd taken to tying them on the front gates. Trouble was, that set her anxiety levels through the roof as she was constantly checking to make sure the local kids hadn't stolen them, or worse still, popped them.

Olga pushed her knife up the sleeve of the hoody. A few flakes of dried blood fluttered from it like macabre confetti.

She reached for the duct tape.

Shit.

Where was it?

She scooted this way and that on the slippery sleeping bag, throwing the bags of bloody clothes out of the way.

It was nowhere to be found.

She froze, pressed her hand to her mouth. An image of the tape lying on the leaf-littered ground in the woods filled her mind. She'd tossed it aside, with the plan of retrieving it, but had forgotten.

Her heart seemed to stop and start in a simultaneous moment. She banged her chest. The tape would be covered in her fingerprints. The police would find it when they found the body, she was absolutely sure of it.

But it was okay.

Her fingerprints weren't on record, so they wouldn't lead the police to her. As long as she kept it that way, kept her nose clean so to speak, she wouldn't get the murder pinned on her.

Taking a deep breath to calm her nerves, she stared at the entrance to the tent. Part of her wanted to wait for the police to leave before she went on the hunt again, but the other part of her was hungry to get the job finished.

Hunger won out.

She stuck her head out of the tent.

Some other band was playing now, and neon-pink and green spotlights were dancing in the sky. The crowd was going wild and singing along—clearly this was a tune they knew and liked.

It was pretty damn awful.

There was a police officer with a dog near the straw bales. Again Olga's heart did a strange skip.

This time she ignored it. Instinct told her to get out now, while she could. Go find her next tormentor and switch the game to the girls.

With an attempt to look as though she were a genuine festivalgoer, she walked towards the main spread of tents. Sure enough, over where Spencer was—or had been, maybe they'd moved his body now—there was a hive of activity. A small group had formed, too. People who'd left the main stage area and discovered something else going on.

But only she knew the secrets of that tent. What had actually happened, the fear in Spencer's eyes, and the way it had taken her several hacks to remove his penis.

With her head down, hair once again falling forward, and the knife held tight, she made her way in the direction of the Portaloos and shower block. She needed to pee.

And if I need to pee, so will Rebecca and Nancy.

She smiled. Surely if she hung around long enough, one of them or both would appear. It was like a lucky dip to see who would get caught first in her web.

The music switched to another song. The lights changed to white and gold. Olga had no idea how anyone could tolerate such whiny tunes.

Slipping into a loo, she relieved herself, being careful with the concealed knife. Inside the small, blue plastic box, the sounds from the generators were loud, as if vibrating through the toilet cubicle.

Once outside, Olga put her hood up and stood half hidden between the shower block and the row of loos. She wished she had a cigarette. She didn't smoke more than a ten-pack a month, it was all she could afford, but right now something to puff on would stop her looking like a murderer waiting for a victim.

A van drove past the tents, its outline just visible on the brow of the hill. The police dogs barked in the distance. She shivered; the temperature was dropping as night took grip.

A glance up at the sky revealed a gap in the clouds. It was shaped like an axe with a long handle, and the stars shining through the hole gave the impression it glinted. Oh, she'd wished her knife had been an axe when taking Charles' hand off. That would have been so much easier.

She tightened her hold on it, the blade cool against her flesh. It hadn't mattered in the end. The job had been done.

The flow of visitors to the toilet was a constant stream. Olga studied everyone, scanning faces in the dim light for Rebecca or Nancy.

After half an hour, she became disheartened. Maybe the girls had gone home or had been taken away by the police for questioning—wouldn't it be hilarious if they were accused of murder. Damn, she should have thought to plant something to put the focus on them.

Next time.

But just as Olga was wondering what to do if neither of the girls appeared, she spotted Nancy.

Petite, wearing minuscule denim shorts and wellies, she trudged, head down towards the loos.

Excitement winged through Olga. Her luck was truly in, fate, demons, and destiny conspiring to help her carry out her revenge.

Nancy stepped up to a loo four down from where Olga stood. She went in and shut the door.

Olga glanced around, then rushed up to the door. She tugged it.

Locked.

Frowning, she fiddled with the lock, struggling to open it from the outside.

"This one is occupied," Nancy called, her small voice weak and pathetic.

Olga didn't reply. She fumbled and fiddled, trying to get it open. The loo would be a perfect place to kill Nancy. If only she could get in there.

"Occupied," Nancy called again. Her voice was throaty, as if she'd been crying.

Good.

Still Olga fiddled.

A bloke went into the loo to the right. He stared at Olga.

She glared at his questioning face. What the hell did it have to do with him?

He shrugged and went inside.

"I'll be out in a minute," Nancy shouted, now sounding exasperated.

"Someone stuck in there?" a girl with plaits to Olga's right said. "Want me to get security to unlock it?"

"No." Olga stepped away. "There's no problem."

Damn it. There were too many curious eyes around.

Hurriedly, she tucked herself back into her hiding place. She'd have to follow Nancy. See where she went and hope it would be somewhere more isolated than this.

Nancy appeared and glanced around as if confused there wasn't someone right outside the door, then walked towards Olga.

Olga slunk deeper into the shadows, dipped her head, and wished her pulse wasn't pounding so loud in her ears—damn thing was competing with the music.

Nancy mooched past, her shoulders slumped and head bowed. It was as if she'd had the sass drained from her, the confidence, the ability to cut a person down with sharp remark and a glare had gone. She was crumbling, the death of Spencer lying heavily on her shoulders.

Well, that was just the start of her pain.

Nancy went into the shower block. She was the first person who had since Olga had been standing there.

Olga followed, glad that her boots weren't audible on the temporary wooden flooring.

Nancy stood at a row of sinks. She leant forward and stared in the mirror. "This can't be happening."

Too bad. It is.

Nancy pulled down first her right eyelid and then her left as if examining the damage her tears had done.

Still vain even in grief.

Olga let the knife slip through the opening of her sleeve. She sent another plea to whatever demons were helping her, asking that they not be disturbed, she only needed a minute or two.

Stepping up behind Nancy, her stomach swirling with excitement, Olga waited to be noticed.

Nancy's concentration was on the mirror. She sniffed and wiped her nose. Checked to see if there was anything between her teeth.

Then she spotted Olga.

She jumped and spun around, hand on her chest. "Shit. You scared me." A flash of recognition crossed her eyes. "Olga."

"I'm surprised you even remember my name." Olga tilted her chin. She was the one with the power now. Nancy's fate was at her mercy.

Nancy's mouth opened, then closed as her attention slid down Olga's body and settled on the glinting knife. "What the hell…?" She glanced over Olga's right shoulder at the entrance.

"Hell, yes, that's where you're going. But don't worry, you can join your boyfriend and his arsehole brother there, so you won't be lonely."

Nancy was pale anyway, but her cheeks turned sheet white. "What have you done?"

"I wouldn't have had to do anything if you hadn't taken those photographs of me." Olga took a step closer, raising the knife, enjoying the dramatic way its blood-soiled blade winked under the lights.

Nancy gasped and pressed against the sink unit. "Please. No."

"No what?"

"Don't…stab me."

"Do you remember when I asked you not to post those pictures?"

Nancy was quiet for a moment, as if the incident had gone from her mind and she was having trouble recollecting it.

"Do you?" Olga asked, a little louder.

"Yes, sorry. I'm really sorry."

"You will be." Olga was close now. If she lunged, she'd be able to stab Nancy right through the heart. Would the blade come out the other side of her chest? It was quite long, and she was small and skinny. Maybe it would.

"Please, no." Nancy stared at the door. "Let me go. I beg you."

"Ahh, another one who begs. Charles did, too. Spencer didn't, I'd put tape over his mouth. He'd said enough. I didn't need to hear any more."

"So you admit it…you killed Spencer?"

"What do you think?"

"Help!" Nancy shouted.

Olga was over her like a flash, the knife pressed against her cheek, the blade entering her flesh in a line.

"Shut up."

Nancy was shaking, a sheen of sweat glossed over her brow.

"You know those funny Chinese monkeys?" Olga said.

"No." A tremor in her voice.

"Yeah, you do. Speak no evil." She touched the end of the blade to Nancy's lips, applied pressure until it pierced the skin. A drop of ruby-red blood appeared.

Nancy shook harder. It seemed she was having to put a lot of effort into keeping still.

Olga appreciated that, having lost her duct tape.

"And see no evil." Olga raised the knife to Nancy's right eye. Like her lip, she pressed a fraction below the lower lid. Another dot of blood appeared.

"I'm so sorry... We all are... It was a stupid joke."

"A joke?" Olga switched eyes, replicated the small cut. Now Nancy looked like she was crying blood; it was kind of cool. "It was more than a prank, it was an evil humiliation of someone who'd never done anything to hurt you."

"You're hurting me. Please...let me go. I'll delete the pictures. I won't tell anyone what you've done. I promise."

"I don't believe you." Olga smiled. "What's the last one...oh yeah, hear no evil." She shoved Nancy's hair behind her right ear, slid the knife into the top crease, leaving a small cut. How easy it was to carve flesh, nowhere near as fibrous as doing a pumpkin at Halloween.

"No..." Nancy glanced at the door again.

"No one is coming to help you. Showering is hardly a popular pastime at this event."

"Let me go."

"As I was saying, hear no evil. And now, Nancy, it's time to start your punishment."

"What, no." Nancy tried to push away.

Olga gripped her left arm, shoved her back, and sliced downwards between her ear and the side of her head.

Blood shot sideways. The ear came almost but not quite off, the fleshy lobe hanging on and the rest dangling.

Nancy screamed, shoved at Olga again.

But Olga was taller, heavier, and determined. She hacked at the remaining bit of ear until it released. The bloody bit of cartilage bounced off Nancy's shoulder and then landed on the floor.

Olga stared at it for a split second, fascinated to see it detached, then a mammoth force shoved at her abdomen. She staggered sideways, the air puffing from her lungs.

Nancy scooted past her, yelping and clutching the hole where her ear had been.

"Fuck," Olga gasped.

But Nancy was fast, too fast, and within seconds was out of sight.

"Damn it." Olga grabbed the ear, shoved it and the knife up her sleeve, and raced to the entrance.

The black night stretched before her. There was no sign of Nancy. This mission had been a failure…a big one.

Chapter Fourteen

Shona walked from the woodland, crunching through twigs, leaves, and stepping over branches as she went. At the fence she met Earle and Julie along with two suited SOCOs carrying boxes of equipment.

"Another one?" Julie said. "Really?"

"Unfortunately." Shona shook her head. "And I'm going to have to leave you to it. This is very much a live case and a friendship group of four. Two are dead. I need to get the others out of here. Fast."

"Go." Julie nodded down the hill. "I've got it. And I'll call you the moment I find anything back at the lab."

"I appreciate that. Come on, Earle."

"You genuinely think the two girls are at risk?" he said. "That it's not someone with just a grudge against the twins."

"I always think the worst."

"Fun way to live." He huffed.

"It keeps me from being disappointed too often."

He fell into step with her.

Lights from the stage flashed through the sky, catching in the cloud cover and misting. She spotted a single opening in the heavy clouds, shaped like a flower attached to a thick stalk with stars filling the petals.

A few tents were being taken down near to where Spencer Cambridge's body had been found. Likely it was people heading home after finding out what had happened. Shona didn't blame them. It was hardly going to be a fun weekend away now.

"We need to question Nancy and Rebecca some more about this Olga Umbridge," she said as they reached the control tent. "Find out why she didn't come to the festival with them. It seems a bit odd if they're all matey enough to have their own secret group on Facebook."

"Good plan. Coffee with your questioning?"

"Please?"

They went into the tent, Earle heading for a huge flask.

Shona stopped dead in her tracks. Rebecca sat alone where she'd left her, but no Nancy.

"What the?" She spun around. Nope. She wasn't in the tent.

Spotting the young female officer, Shona marched up to her. "Where is the other girl?" She pointed at Rebecca. "I left two with you."

"She's gone to the toilet?" The officer bit on her bottom lip and wrung her hands. Shifted from one foot to the other.

"On her fucking own!" Shona reached up and tightened her ponytail so hard her scalp stung. "Jesus Christ, I asked you if you had this, and you said yes."

"I'm sorry, ma'am I thought you meant getting the scarf to the dog handlers."

"Well, yes, that as well as watching the girls."

"I took the scarf and when I came back, Nancy had gone. Rebecca says she went to the toilet."

"Bloody hell."

"You okay?" Earle was at her side holding a mug.

"No." Shona took it. Sipped. Burnt her tongue. "Fuck!" She pointed at the door. "Go and find her, Sergeant. Now. Get a few other uniforms, if there are any going spare. I want the girl back here within the next sixty seconds."

"Yes, ma'am." She shot from the tent.

"Can you believe it?" Shona stared up at Earle. "That wouldn't have happened at the Met."

"This isn't the Met." He sipped his coffee.

"Right now, with all these murders, stabbings, it feels like it." She cautiously took another drink of coffee. Her heart was hammering. If something had happened to Nancy Braithwaite while she was supposed to be in police care, all hell would break loose. And Fletcher...he'd bust a blood vessel, most likely.

"We need to fill Fletcher in," Shona said. "I'll call him as soon as I've spoken to Rebecca, get the okay to shut this event down. Hopefully Nancy will be back by then and I won't have to confess we lost her."

"Good plan." He paused. "You going to tell her about Charles' body being found in the woods?"

"Not yet. I need to get some sense out of her."

They stepped over to Rebecca who was spinning a damp tissue in her hands. Small fibres were breaking off and salting her legs.

"Hey," Shona said, taking a seat and plucking her phone out of her pocket. "You okay?"

"Not really." She sniffed. "I'm worried about Charles. And it's so awful about Spencer. I can't believe it's true."

"I know this is really, really hard for you, but I need to ask you a few questions about this girl." Shona brought her phone to life and found the picture of Olga. "You know her, right?"

Rebecca glanced at the screen, frowned, and looked away.

"Is that a yes?" Shona asked.

Rebecca nodded.

"I believe it's Olga Umbridge, am I correct?"

Another nod.

"A friend of yours?"

"Not really."

"So how do you know her?"

"We're in college together." She dabbed her nose.

"But you hang out?"

"No." She studied the picture again and scowled. "I mean look at her, she's weird. Not the sort of person I'd hang out with."

Earle raised his eyebrows at Shona.

She did the same back, then, "Does she always dress like this?"

"Yes, she's a Goth, creepy with it."

"So you don't like her."

"I don't know her." She pointed at the door. "Can I go now?"

"No, we want you to stay here."

"Why." She stood. "Am I under arrest?"

"Of course not." Shona remained seated but rested her hand on Rebecca's arm. "We want to keep you safe."

"Safe?"

"Yes. I think you'll agree that has to be a priority."

She swallowed, closed her eyes, and sat. "Okay." She set her attention on Earle and then Shona. "But I've never had anything to do with Olga Umbridge. She's nothing to me."

Shona had questioned enough people to be able to spot the small micro-expressions—a tiny sneer, glance to the left, tensed jawline—to know there was something Rebecca wasn't telling them. "She's nothing to you. Not a friend and not a…"

"Nothing."

"So not an enemy. Not someone who would want to hurt Spencer, Charles, you, or Nancy?"

"No, she's a dippy cow. Wouldn't have it in her."

"Okay." Shona's phone rang, the image of Olga disappearing and in its place Andy's name.

"Excuse me for a minute." She stood and stepped away.

"Ma'am, it's Andy, I'm still at the station."

"Great, what have you got?"

"I've dug around on Facebook, gone back a month. Seems one of the Cambridge twins, Charles, along with Rebecca Smith-Brown and Nancy Braithwaite, posted several, let's call them rather embarrassing images of Olga Umbridge."

"Go on."

He cleared his throat. "They've all got a lot of friends, over a thousand each. Olga, on the other hand, has just one, a girl called Stacey. She also has no timeline posts and one image of herself that I sent you, and a graveyard as her cover picture. So the three of them posting had a ton of comments, I've read over two hundred, not one of them is nice. In fact, the majority are brutal."

Shona rubbed her temple. "Poor girl."

"Exactly. I'll send you the images."

"Thanks."

"Do you want the comments?"

"No, not at the moment." She ended the call.

Earle was at her side. "What have you got?"

"This little group, it seems, have been rather wicked to Olga," she said quietly.

"Which gives her motive."

Shona said nothing. She didn't want to think a young woman was capable of the mutilations she'd witnessed.

But anything was possible. Weird shit happened. Life was one crazy roller coaster.

Her phone came to life again. Pictures sent from Andy. She opened them.

A shockingly bright image of a girl on her knees, clothing around her ankles, and apparently having oral sex.

"Shit," Earle muttered, leaning in. "Who's the bloke? With the blurred-out face."

"I'm guessing Spencer Cambridge. What do you think?"

He was quiet for a moment. "I agree. And his twin took the picture?"

"Most likely." She scrolled through several more images. Each degrading, humiliating, and shocking. It was clear they were all of Olga Umbridge, and it was also blatantly obvious by her scared eyes and posture she was distressed at the time they were taken.

"So they snapped these and then Charles and Rebecca and Nancy spread them around Facebook," Shona said. "Spencer was the one who, and I'm guessing here, lured her into the situation."

Earle glanced at Rebecca. "No wonder she wasn't forthcoming. What they did was horrible."

"She bloody well will be now." Shona marched over to her and sat. She thrust her phone in front of Rebecca. "Can you explain these images?"

"What?" She gasped. "Who is that?"

"You know who it is."

"I don't."

"Several of these pictures were on your Facebook timeline. You took them." Shona didn't know that for sure but decided it was worth the risk to push on with, "And we can prove it."

"It's...it's Olga Umbridge." Rebecca gulped.

"And where were these photographs taken?"

"At The Moorhouse, back at home, Lincoln."

"And you asked her permission before taking them? Before posting them on a public social media platform?"

She shook her head. Her eyes welled up with tears.

"Well?" Shona said.

"No. I...we didn't ask her."

"Pretty cruel, don't you think?" Shona frowned. "Judging by the compromising position."

"It was...supposed to be for a laugh, and we didn't think Facebook would let us keep them up anyway. Usually stuff like that gets banned."

"She doesn't give the impression that she's laughing." Shona flicked to the image of Olga trying to cover her nakedness. "In fact, she appears horrified, distraught, scared."

"It was Spencer's idea. He said he could charm the knickers off any girl, even the weirdest ones."

"And the rest of you went along with it?"

"I suppose." She shrugged and looked at the door. "When will Charles be here? And where's Nancy? She's been a long time."

"To be honest, I'm worried about Nancy. I have officers out searching for her."

She pressed her hand to her mouth, her eyes widening. "Do you think someone might hurt her? Or Charles, what about him?"

"Someone." Shona waggled the phone. "What if that someone is Olga Umbridge? What if you upset her so much with your nasty trick that she's taking revenge on all of you?"

"She wouldn't. She hardly even speaks. She..." Rebecca appeared shocked at the suggestion. "She's just a...girl."

"I would imagine she was a very hurt girl after the world and his wife saw those pictures. What you did was mean, very mean, Rebecca."

"I know." Her face crumpled. "I wish we hadn't now, really I do."

"It's too late for that." Shona stood and drew up Andy's number.

I really need contact details for Olga Umbridge ASAP.

She returned to her coffee, took a drink. It was cooler now. Glancing at the door, she suppressed a sense of doom. Nancy should have been found by now. Shit. Fletcher was going to hit the roof, which wasn't good when she was so new on the job.

Her phone came to life. A contact phone number and address for Olga. A place called Brayton in Lincolnshire.

She hit call on the number and stepped out of Rebecca's earshot. It was a landline, and after several rings it was answered by a female.

"Hello, is that Olga Umbridge?"

"Is that you Olga?"

"No, it's DI Shona Williams calling from Ironash. Whom am I speaking to please?"

"Mrs Umbridge...do I know you?"

"No, madam, but I need to speak to your daughter, Olga."

"My daughter? Oh, she's not here, she's supposed to be calling, though, that's why I thought you were her. But I should go...the balloons need my attention, it's so dark you see, a little windy, too. The white ones don't like the wind, not at all."

Balloons?

"So Olga isn't at home?" Shona asked.

"No. I have to go, sorry."

"Please, I won't keep you long, Mrs Umbridge," Shona went on quickly. "I just need to ask you if you know where Olga is?"

"Oh yes, she's gone to a concert, her first one. Left me a nice lasagne, she did, just finished it. I had pickles and mushy peas with it, went rather nice. You tried that?"

"Er, no. Any idea which concert?" Did she mean festival?

"No, she's all grown up now, my Olga, I don't ask her questions." She paused. "She did say it was in a field, though, and she took the tent to sleep in."

Bloody hell, so she is here.

Shona set her attention on Earle who was studying her intently. She nodded and mouthed 'she's here'.

His jaw tensed, and he looked at the entrance.

"What colour tent does she have?" Shona asked.

"Black, and it's round, quite nice it is, balloon-shaped. Now I really must go. I've neglected the outdoor balloons for too long. Excuse me."

The line went dead.

"Bloody hell," Shona muttered to Earle. "She's here. A black domed tent." She clicked her fingers as thoughts rushed through her brain. They needed to search for her, now, quickly. But there were so many tents, and the officers were already busy with two murder scenes and searching for Nancy.

They needed help.

"I have to call Fletcher. Get this event shut down and call in more manpower."

"What do you want me to do?"

"Coordinate a wider search and—"

Shona's words were cut off as a rush of energy burst through the entrance.

A young woman, clutching the side of her blood-streaked head, staggered in, wailing.

"Nancy." Shona rushed to her.

Earle, too.

"It's her. It's her," Nancy cried, sinking to her knees, her eyes wide and terrified.

"Get a paramedic in here. Now!" Earle bellowed.

Two uniforms rushed off.

Shona reached for the young woman. Her face was pale, blood dripped from her chin, and she had a slicing cut over her cheek. Her shoulder, arm, and chest were soaked red. "What do you mean? Who is it?"

"Olga. Olga Umbridge."

"No!" Rebecca jumped up. "It can't be."

Nancy was sobbing. Her right hand was full of blood, and a jagged bit of hair and scalp poked through her fingers. "Yes, it's her, she…she's here and she…cut off my ear." She moved her hand. A pulse of blood shot from an open vein and landed on the ground by Earle's boot.

"Here, press this on it." Shona snatched a wad of blue roll from an officer standing to her right. "Apply pressure."

Nancy did as she was asked, her entire arm shaking. "You have to find her, she's mad. She's got a knife, a big one."

"Olga Umbridge, you're sure?" Shona asked.

"Yes. She's here, dressed all in black, creepy, mad." She turned to Rebecca. "She said she'd killed Spencer, and I think she's hurt Charles, too."

"What?" Rebecca's mouth fell open. "No, not Charles as well. No…" She looked around wildly. "This can't be happening."

"I told you," Nancy said, "that we went too far putting those pictures online." She grimaced in pain. "We should have just had a laugh over them ourselves."

Rebecca closed her eyes and cried—a deep, regretful, agony-riddled wail.

"We shouldn't have done that to her." Nancy shook her head. "Because now she wants to kill us all."

A paramedic rushed in, scooting to his knees and dumping a black bag on the ground. "Okay, okay, let's have a peep at this. You're going to be okay, young lady."

Shona stood. She turned to Earle. "Let's get searching. How many domed black tents can there be?"

Chapter Fifteen

Olga left the shower block and ran back to her tent, her breaths coming quick and sharp as she turned past the straw bales. The music was still thudding, banging through the air and vibrating into her body.

She opened the zip on the entrance to her tent—her hands peppered with blood spots—and dived inside. Quickly, she shut it again, sealing herself away from the noise, the lights, the crowds, the evil people who'd made her become what she had.

Pressing the heels of her hands to her eyes, she groaned and rocked backwards and forwards. Nancy had escaped her clutches, taken off into the darkness and disappeared in the swell of people.

Without her ear.

Olga suddenly remembered the bloody piece of anatomy. She reached into her hoody sleeve and retrieved it.

She set it on the sleeping bag and studied it. She'd never considered before how strange an ear looked when it wasn't attached to a head. The fibrous flesh was raggedy where she'd hacked at it—this hadn't been a clean cut. The fleshy little lobe still had the small diamond stud piercing in it.

Olga poked the stud with her fingernail. Maybe it would be worth something. Nancy's parents were rich, so it was likely to be real. If she sold it, perhaps she could recoup the price of the festival ticket. Yes, that was what she'd do. Sell it. Get her money back. Then she'd rebuy her vinyls.

Reaching for the dolls that represented her victims, she lay them on the sleeping bag, next to the ear. Spencer with his spongy material erupting from his groin. Charles minus his hands. Nancy's face stabbed out, and Rebecca's head cut off.

"My revenge will soon be complete," she muttered, twisting the Rebecca doll so the torso did a full turn. "You can't escape me, Nancy and Rebecca, I am coming for you."

She held in a manic giggle, knowing how scared they would be now. How humiliated Nancy would be to have an ear missing.

Would they be sad that their stupid boyfriends were dead? She doubted it. People like Nancy and Rebecca only thought of themselves—they only loved themselves. But they would be the talk of the college now. And not in a good way. That would serve them right.

I'll get a picture of Nancy without her ear and post it.

The manic giggle returned.

When she'd settled her mirth, Olga reached for a packet of Quavers and started munching, crumbs spilling from her mouth.

It dawned on her that she'd have to leave the festival soon. Her chance for killing Rebecca and Nancy had slipped by.

Damn you, Nancy, for running away.

Nancy would have told Rebecca that they were being hunted. No doubt they'd drive home. Escape.

"But that's okay. There'll be opportunities in the future." Olga smiled at that. The girls attended the gym in town, and the underground car park was dark and quiet. Not only that, she'd found out Rebecca's address, a big old house standing all alone, just the sort used in horror movies because it was isolated and had multiple nooks and crannies for a murderer to hide in.

Yes, she'd get them both. She'd wait, bide her time. The trip to the festival had been a success, she'd got two of her targets. And in all honesty, she'd expected the boys to be the hardest to overcome. Seemed she had quite a talent for killing and was stronger and more efficient than she'd thought. She'd tell the career advice officer that when she next saw her.

I've chosen my subject for uni, Miss Drake...murder.

She laughed again, yellow Quaver flakes falling like snow onto the dolls and the ear.

The music changed, and she looked at the door. This was a slower song. After upending the crisp packet to get out the last crumbs, she tossed it aside and wrapped her arms around herself. She rocked back and forth to the music, memories of Spencer's scared eyes and Charles' wails of agony slipping into her mind. Again she chuckled. It was their shock that amused her. They really couldn't believe weirdo Olga Umbridge had them at her mercy. That their lives were going to be ended by the Goth-fuck-freak they'd tormented so wickedly.

Well, she'd tormented them right back. She'd taught them the error of their ways. They'd paid the ultimate price.

Death.

* * *

Olga's photograph and the description of the tent had gone out to all ground officers and security. Anyone who wasn't keeping a crime scene secure was searching or manning the perimeter.

Shona dialled up Fletcher, wincing at the time. It was gone midnight.

He answered, sounding sleepy.

"Sir, sorry to bother you." She glanced left and right, scanning tents. Earle was at her side, doing the same while they walked.

"No apologies, I'm guessing it's important if you're calling, DI Williams."

"Yes. There's been two deaths, suspected murders, at the festival."

"Shit, really?" He sounded wide awake now.

"Twins, from the Lincoln area. Spencer and Charles Cambridge." Damn it. This was feeling like a needle-in-a-haystack search. There were tents everywhere.

"And the perpetrator?"

"We have a suspect, an Olga Umbridge, known to them at college."

"A girl." He paused. "And her whereabouts?"

"I suspect she's here." She pointed at a black tent to her right.

"I'll take a peek." Earle said.

"And, sir, there are two girls in the friendship group. One has been attacked by Olga."

"So find this Olga, now."

"Yes, sir. I need permission to shut this festival down, for tonight at least."

"Do it. Do whatever you need to. I'll be there as soon as I can."

Shona watched Earle flash his torch into the tent. He spoke, then nodded and stood.

"Not this one," he said.

"Thank you, sir." Shona returned her attention to the call. "The press are likely to get wind of it soon."

"Naturally." He tutted, then, "Leave shutting the festival down to me. I'll get onto the organiser right now and I'll fend off the press. If this Olga Umbridge is there, concentrate on finding her, make that your priority, Detective."

"Yes, sir. Thank you. I'll update you as soon as we have anything."

"And keep those two girls under police protection."

She paused. "Absolutely, sir." She ended the call, stomping up the hill with Earle. Within a few seconds, her phone rang again.

"Sergeant Nicols, have you got something?"

"Yes, ma'am. Reports of a lone tent matching the description, to the west of the field near the woods. It's set back, behind some straw bales."

"Okay, I'm on my way." She did a thumbs-up sign to Earle.

He nodded, his mouth a tight, serious line.

"And don't let anyone approach, Sergeant. She's got a knife and goodness knows what else. We have to presume she's dangerous and maybe more so when she realises she's cornered."

"Yes, ma'am, I'll give that order."

Shona ended the call.

"Do that up." Earle pointed at the flapping Velcro on her stab vest.

"Thanks." She tightened it. She'd been in such a rush to get searching when she'd shrugged it on. "Near the straw bales. They don't know if she's in there or not."

"What do you think?"

"I'd say it's fifty-fifty. If she's determined to harm Rebecca and Nancy then she'll still be around. If she's spooked because Nancy knows what she's up to, she could have taken off. And with those woods…"

"We'll find her."

"Yes." Shona nodded. "We will."

We have to.

They broke into a run, the beams from their torches bouncing on the ground. The straw bales came into view, looming high in the darkness. Beyond them the stretch of the woodland, the treetops piercing the black sky.

It became clear there were several officers standing around. The police dogs, too. One of them barked at Shona and Earle's rapid approach.

"Ma'am," a tall officer said, using his torch to indicate the location of the tent. "There's been no movement, but there does seem to be a light on in there. A torch hanging from the roof pole perhaps."

"Okay, thanks, and be ready, she's armed with a knife and dangerous." She nodded at the dog handlers. "And if she's not in there, we're going to need a search."

"Yes, ma'am. Dogs are ready."

"Very good." She turned to Earle. "You with me?"

"Do you need to ask?" He squeezed her arm.

She smiled, even though her heart was pounding, not just from their run up the hill but also with anticipation. Was Olga Umbridge in that tent? And if so, what the hell was she doing, and, more to the point, what would she do when they pulled open the entrance?

* * *

Olga looked up. A dog was barking nearby.

She liked dogs. Perhaps she'd find it and pet it.

She stroked her fingertip over the top curve of Nancy's ear. It felt weird, not like flesh anymore, but rubber. It was pale, too, a sickly shade of creamy white.

Suddenly the drumbeat ceased, the final note tinkling through the air.

Quiet.

The music had gone off.

Voices.

There's voices nearby. Who?

For a moment she hoped it was Nancy and Rebecca. If they'd come to find her then it would save her a job of searching for them.

She stroked the ear again. Nancy would want it back. Likely she'd think it could be sewn on. What a stupid idea. But then Nancy was stupid. All she thought about was makeup, clothes, and her idiot boyfriend.

Boyfriend no more.

"Olga Umbridge." A female voice. "This is the police. Come out of the tent."

Olga snatched in a breath and snapped her attention to the entrance.

The police. What the hell were they doing here? How had they found her? Her little tent was a safe haven, camouflaged in the darkness, and she'd left nothing outside it, not even her boots this time.

She swallowed, a tight lump seeming to have formed in her throat. Her heart rated sped up, and her pulse thudded in her temples. A strange twist caught in her belly.

Quickly, she reached up and switched off the torch hanging above her head.

Instantly an image of Spencer sprawled out and bleeding jumped into her mind. He was there, in the darkness with her. Scared eyes, tape over his mouth, battling his binds.

"Olga Umbridge, we know you're in there. We need to talk to you. Come out of the tent."

She shook, a full head-to-toe rattle.

"My name is DI Williams, we just have a few questions for you."

Olga's teeth chattered; it was cold, so cold now. She pulled her sleeves over her hands and rocked back and forth. Her hair hung forward, her hood stroking the back of her head.

"I'm going to open the door to the tent."

The female voice was closer now. Much closer. Just outside, in fact.

Olga closed her eyes. Maybe she'd go away if she didn't answer. This was her tent after all. Her property. Her territory.

The metallic whiz of the zip created a whimper in Olga's chest. It caught in her nostrils, and she wiped at the end of her nose with her sleeve. The sensation of being stalked was like a rash going over her skin.

On and on the zip slid upwards. It was as if this DI Williams was a little afraid, a little unsure of what she might find.

Olga opened her eyes as a flash of light seared over her lids.

It was too bright, so she focused on what was laid before her.

The voodoo dolls. The bloodstained carving knife. The mangled ear.

"Jesus Christ." A deep male voice.

A sharp inhalation. "Olga, we need you to step out of the tent."

Olga looked up at the woman who'd spoken. She was pretty with blonde hair, could have been one of Nancy or Rebecca's crowd. But on closer inspection it was clear she was older, and her eyes had a sharp intelligence about them.

Olga rocked back and forth, hugging her arms around herself. "They hurt me."

"I know they did. Please, come out of the tent so we can talk about this."

"They hurt me first. They..." A sob trapped the rest of her words.

"I understand. What they did was cruel." She paused as the knife was removed by a big gloved hand belonging to the black man at her side. "But hurting them back, killing, it wasn't the answer."

"So what was?"

"Do you have any other knives?"

"No, just that one, from the kitchen at home. Mum wouldn't miss it. She doesn't cook, see."

The woman frowned, as though understanding. "Let's get you out of this tent so we can talk."

Olga nodded. Suddenly the tent didn't feel so nice anymore. It was cold, a bit smelly, too, what with the bags of bloody clothes.

"Okay. I'll come out." She pushed her fingers from her sleeve.

The woman pulled back the opening. "This way."

Olga emerged from the tent. The stage in the distance was silent and lit up, as though engineers were deconstructing it. The straw bales loomed to her right. And beside them a gaggle of policemen and dogs were staring at her.

A woman in a strange white suit was holding the bagged carving knife and staring at Olga as though confused and fascinated at the same time.

"I had to do it," Olga directed at her. "I had to have my revenge. They had to learn they can't treat me that way. I'm different, yeah, but that doesn't mean I can be humiliated, treated like shit. My mother has had that all of her life, I don't want that, too."

"Olga Umbridge," the pretty woman said. "You are under arrest on suspicion of the murder of Spencer Cambridge, Charles Cambridge, and for grievous bodily harm to Nancy Braithwaite. You do not have to say anything, but it may harm your defence if you do not mention when questioned something which you later rely on in court. Anything you do say may be given in evidence."

"Arrest." Olga gasped as her arms were dragged behind her back. Something tightened around her wrists, hard and strong, snapping them together. She squirmed and battled the entrapment. "But I didn't do anything wrong."

Chapter Sixteen

Shona watched as Earle gripped Olga Umbridge by the upper arm, preventing her from fleeing into the darkness. Not that she'd get very far with all the uniforms and dogs around.

But it was clear that was what she wanted to do. Get away from them all.

What was also evident was her madness. As crazy as her mother had been when Shona had spoken to her on the phone and she'd been harping on about balloons.

Had she been this mad before the wicked game that had been played out at her expense, or had that been the cause of it? Being the laughing stock of college, and with such vitriol hate, venomous scorn, couldn't have been easy and may have tipped her over the edge of a psychotic precipice.

Shona reckoned they'd find out during the trial. Which wouldn't be a long one. With all the evidence, including the murder weapon and Nancy's hacked off ear, Olga Umbridge wouldn't have a leg to stand on. The question would be, should she go to regular prison or Southall?

Shona would put money on Southall, the secure psychiatric unit, and for a very long time.

"Take her away." Shona nodded at the tall uniformed officer who'd met them at the brow of the hill. "With as little a scene as possible. I'm expecting the press to get hold of this soon."

"Yes, ma'am."

Earle handed Olga to the uniform, who set off at a brisk march with Olga at his side, three other officers and the dogs also in tow.

"Set up a perimeter around this tent." Shona drew an imaginary line. "So SOCO can do their work." She nodded at Julie. "There's a lot in there, including the ear."

"Pardon." Julie laughed. "Sorry, couldn't resist."

Shona chuckled then sighed. She looked up at Earle. "This hasn't been the fun festival it should have been."

"Nope. But it's just as well we swung by earlier, got the lay of the land."

"Yes, you're right." Her phone went; it was Sergeant Nicols. "Sergeant Nicols, we have the suspect in custody," Shona said.

"Good, yes, I just heard. But..."

"But?" Shona frowned. "But what?"

"You said you wanted to be informed of anything untoward."

"Yes." Shona started walking around the straw bales. "What is it?"

"I have two festivalgoers in the control tent. Women. One is out of it, spaced, like she's high. But her friend says they haven't taken anything. Not even a glass of wine."

"Do you think she's telling the truth?"

"Yes, I've got a paramedic in here now. He's concerned. Lina Davis aged seventeen, that's the one out of it, her pupils are pinpoint, she's limp, wobbly as though not in command of her body, and she's not making any sense. He agrees with me, there's no alcohol on her breath and certainly no whiff of weed."

"It could be anything, get her to hospital."

"Ambulance is just being organised."

Shona was quiet, sensing there was more.

"The friend," Nicols went on, "said she saw a male put something in Lina's drink—it was a can of cola apparently."

Shona stopped walking, her feet seeming to root to the ground and a strange jelly sensation coming over her knees.

The Asian. I saw him here...earlier.

"Description...of the male."

"She only saw him from behind. Medium height, dark hair, tanned, red t-shirt, that's all she's got."

"Fuck."

"Ma'am?"

"Sorry. Go on."

"He sidled up behind Lina, didn't speak to her or anything, just tampered with the cola, then slipped into the crowd."

"To watch and wait."

"That's what I thought. Luckily, Lina has a good friend to look out for her and bring her to safety."

Earle was at Shona's side, a questioning frown ploughing over his brow.

"We'll be there in a few minutes, but if the ambulance arrives, let them take the victim."

"Yes, ma'am."

Shona hung up. She pulled in a deep breath, letting the cool night air coat her throat and windpipe. Her heart was rattling against her chest, and nausea twisted her guts.

But this is why I came back to Ironash.

Be strong. Follow the trail.

She folded her arms tight around her chest, glanced around, then addressed Earle. "A young woman has been slipped a roofie. Luckily her friend spotted the crime the moment it happened and took the victim straight to safety."

"Shit." Earle studied the throng of people dismantling tents. "Rohypnol strikes again."

"What do you mean?"

"There's been a few attacks while I've been a detective here in Ironash."

"I haven't had a chance to familiarise myself with all the cases." Damn it, it was next week's job, to study the others. "Leads?"

"Frustratingly, no. Feels like the perpetrators have read the manual on how to get away with rape."

"They probably have, these things are on the web now." Shona gritted her teeth. She knew. She'd found them for herself. "Come on, let's go talk to the friend, while it's fresh in her memory."

"Good idea."

They marched into the sea of tents now in a state of disassembly. The atmosphere was tense, people working quickly.

Murder.

Stabbed.

Dead.

Might be us next.

Knife.

All words Shona heard as she walked. The only consolation was these people would be safe from Olga Umbridge while they packed up and made their way home.

To her right she spotted a reporter, microphone in hand, a cameraman behind him.

Her heart sank. She hoped no names would be released until the twins' parents had been spoken to. In fact, she should double-check on that. She pulled out her phone to call Fletcher.

It was then she saw him.

Dark jeans. Boots. Red t-shirt. Hair shiny, as though gelled or greasy. But it was the thick brow that her focus zoned in on. It was like being a radar set out to seek him.

He was walking with his hands in his pockets, seeming to study the people around him who, unlike him, were all busy with their tasks.

Adrenaline pumped into her system. She broke into a run. He was twenty yards away, wandering in the opposite direction.

"Shona," Earle called.

She ignored him. She had to catch this man. He'd drugged her. He'd drugged a girl tonight. He had to be stopped, and this was her chance before he disappeared yet again.

Shona leapt over a burnt-out campfire, scooted around a pile of holdalls and cool boxes, then shoulder barged a young man draining a can of cider.

She sensed Earle behind her but raced ahead. The medley of emotions raging inside her fought for attention, but mostly it was rage—rage and urgency.

When she was only ten feet from him, he turned. His expression flashed with surprise for a brief second, then he shot into a sprint.

"Stop. You. Police!"

He kept on going.

But Shona was going full pelt, and she had momentum on her side. One more step.

She threw herself into the air, wrapping her arms around his hips, her body weight driving into his.

Although he was heavier than her, he succumbed and hit the deck.

Unfortunately, he landed fighting. He twisted and threw a punch her way, aiming for her face.

She dodged it and blocked a second blow. Pinned his left arm to the ground, his wrist bent at an unnatural angle and trapped there.

He growled and bucked beneath her, twisting to shake her off.

Being so close to him sent a rise of bile into her mouth. She hissed out a breath. "Stop resisting arrest."

"Fuck off. I haven't done anything wrong." He kicked, ramming his knees into her back.

The air huffed from Shona's lungs, and she was flung forward, closer to him.

She curled her free hand around his throat, blocking the airflow, and stared into his eyes.

Instantly he stilled. His eyes widened, and his tongue stuck out. She could see the ugly gap in his top front teeth.

"You have done something wrong, something criminal and vile, and you know it, you piece of shit." She tightened her grip. "And now it's time to pay."

He made a weird croaking sound and clawed at her wrist.

hed her jaw, happy to watch the life drain from him.

"I've got it." Earle was at her side. "Shona."

All she needed was another minute.

"Stop." Earle wrapped his arm around her waist, pulled her away.

Every instinct was to complete the job, fight Earle, too. But the voice of common sense rang through her brain. Quiet at first but getting louder as she stood.

The Asian gripped his throat and dragged in air. He stared at her, but there didn't appear to be any recognition in his eyes. She'd shaken him up with her sudden attack.

"Arrest him," she said, pointing, "He's the one who slipped the date rape drug to the girl."

Earle produced a pair of handcuffs, squatted, and snapped them on. He twisted to look up at Shona. "How do you know?"

"I just do." She stepped back, shoved her shaking hands into her pockets and turned away, unable to look at his face. "Believe me, I just do."

Chapter Seventeen

"I'll see you later." Shona grabbed a muesli bar and waved at her parents who were in their dressing gowns in the kitchen.

"Sweetheart, perhaps you could go in later today, you were out at the festival until goodness knows what hour," her mother said.

"Yes, and there's still unfinished business." She nodded at her father. "Have a good day at the golf course."

"I will." He frowned. "You okay?"

"Yes." She smiled. "And I'll be even better later if I can make today go how I want it to."

She headed out of the door, car keys in hand. With the Asian—Samri Laghari—in custody, she'd never been so close to justice for herself, Nicola, and Tina. Now it was just a case of getting him identified and questioning him until he slipped up.

Unfortunately, there hadn't been any evidence of drugs on him, but that didn't prove his innocence. Likely he only took one dose to the festival—that was all he needed to slip one poor unsuspecting girl to have his sick night of fun.

She arrived at Ironash Police Station and parked next to Earle's big car. She was glad he was here. She was becoming used to his solid presence and his ability to stay cool when things heated up.

"Morning," he said, rising from his seat when she entered the office. "Fletcher is waiting for us."

Shona frowned and dumped her bag in her drawer next to the sketch of Samri Laghari. Her intention had been to get straight down to the interrogation room.

"And," Earle went on, "last night's victim."

"Her name is Lina Davis."

He nodded. "Lina Davis is due in at ten with her friend. She was discharged from hospital this morning."

"So the drug has left her body."

"Seems that way."

Shona nodded. Roofies were notoriously quick to leave the bloodstream via urine, which was why perpetrators of the crime acted quickly, had their fun, then dumped the victims.

Bastards.

"Okay, let's go and see Fletcher then head down to interrogation."

Earle nodded and gestured for her to go first.

Fletcher was staring out of his office window, hands on his hips.

"Good morning, sir," Shona said.

Earle shut the door.

"The festival turned into a nightmare." He shook his head. "The press have agreed to hold off until the twins' parents have landed at Heathrow and identified the bodies."

"They know about their sons?"

He closed his eyes and scrubbed his palm over the nape of his neck. "I told them last night." He dropped his hand to his side and set his attention on his phone. "I hate doing that by phone call, but what choice did I have?"

"None, sir. They were in Austria." Shona was grateful her new boss hadn't shirked the very worst of jobs.

"And," Fletcher went on, "Olga Umbridge has had an emergency psychiatric evaluation." He paused. "And I'm afraid we won't be able to question her while she's in the midst of a psychotic episode."

"So she's unfit," Shona clarified, not at all surprised.

"Yes, but she's confessed in front of witnesses multiple times from what I gather."

"Yeah," Earle said, "she as good as admitted it when we arrested her."

Fletcher held out his hands. "What possesses people? Honestly?"

"She was horribly provoked," Shona said, "and with some pretty serious mental health issues and a very complex home life, that all added up to one shitstorm of violence." Shona pulled a face, remembering the state of the bodies and Nancy's amputated ear. "She was going to kill the two girls involved, too. At least she didn't get that far."

"Facebook has a lot to answer for. So much for their anti-bullying policies."

"I suppose it's too big to police." Shona shrugged.

"And would we get away with saying that about our district?" Fletcher tutted.

"No, sir." Shona paused. "I'd like to say we should be thankful for small mercies in that the girls weren't killed by Olga, but we still have two murdered young men who had their whole lives in front of them."

Much the same as Nicola and Tina had.

Shona glanced at the door.

"Somewhere to be?" Fletcher asked.

"Yes, we brought in a man last night on suspicion of drugging a girl's drink. I'm keen to question him and get a formal identification."

"Ah, yes, I noticed that report. Good, go and do that."

"Yes, sir."

Shona and Earle went from the room.

Earle paused at the coffee. "Want one?"

"Yes, thanks." She was itching to get face to face with Samri Laghari, have him confess, but knew she had to keep her cool. This wasn't the time to go hell for leather. Her fury and frustration had nearly got the better of her the night before. She'd only just reined it in, and if Earle hadn't been there…

She pulled in a deep breath and took the coffee Earle handed her. They made their way to the lift.

"This Samri," Earle said while they waited for the lift. "You were pretty sure he had something to do with the drug case when you chased him down."

"Yes."

"How?"

She hesitated. He was digging, pushing. She couldn't blame him. But this wasn't the time to tell Earle how she knew—there might never be a time. This was her business, her past. She was on a mission that had been held close to her heart for years. She'd shaken the shame of it—with therapy—moved on, but still...it was hers. "He matched the description."

"Which was?"

"Medium height, red t-shirt, black hair."

Earle kind of chuckled, but it didn't hold humour. "That fits a lot of the male festivalgoers."

She frowned. "I just had a feeling...okay?"

"A hunch?"

"What? You don't believe in them?"

He held up his free hand as if in surrender. "Hey, whatever floats your boat. What I was going to say was you handled him well when he was on the ground. The man really wanted to get away. He was fighting back."

"Another sign he's guilty."

Earle was quiet as they stepped into the lift. The doors closed. "You know a bit of jiujitsu then?"

"And karate. Sensible in this line of work."

"I agree." He paused. "Laghari is probably twice your weight."

He didn't need to finish the sentence for Shona to know what he was going to say...what he was thinking.

And you could have killed him.

"I'm a black belt," she confessed. "I view the belt like a safety net, self-defence, it comes in handy when a punch is thrown my way."

Earle nodded. "And here was me thinking you only liked me because I provided the muscle."

"I like you for many reasons, Earle, but muscle isn't needed when there's technical know-how." She jabbed him with her elbow and smiled. "Though I'm sure, going forward, there's going to be times I'm damn grateful for your fast legs and muscle. Not to mention height."

He grinned and sipped his coffee.

"What?" she asked, sensing he was holding something back.

"People make a mistake when they underestimate you, Shona."

It hadn't been said as a question, so she didn't reply. She'd let Earle into some of her confidence, about her karate, and that felt right. He was a good man. She was lucky to have him at her side now she was here in Ironash.

They went into the interrogation room where Samri Laghari was seated on a hard plastic chair at a table that had been chained to the floor. He wasn't cuffed now and held a plastic cup of water.

"What the hell am I doing here?" he said with a snarl. "If you can't charge me with something, which you can't, let me go."

"Be quiet," Shona said, again looking for recognition in his eyes. There was none. "No talking until we have the tape running."

Earle stepped in and shut the door.

Samri glared at each of them in turn.

Shona's heart was thumping, and she was suppressing images of Samri's face looming before her in a different time and place. They weren't whole images, just fragments, snippets, like a subliminal flash, but they were there. And her hypnosis meant she was able to see them.

But this wasn't about her or that night. This was about Lina Davis.

She sat and hit start on the tape recorder. "Interview with Samri Laghari, DI Williams and DS Montague present."

"I want a solicitor," Samri said, crushing the plastic cup and shoving it over the table.

"Why, what have you done wrong?" Shona asked.

"Nothing." He pointed at the door. "And I need to go. I have work to do."

"Where do you work?"

"None of your business."

"Failing to answer questions will keep you here longer," Earle said, sitting back and folding his arms. His biceps bulged against his short-sleeved white shirt.

Samri glared at him. "I'm a delivery driver."

"For what company?" Shona asked.

"My own, I've got contacts."

"Who?"

His frown deepened, the ugly monobrow sinking so low it almost covered his mean, narrowed brown eyes. "Small independent shops, cafés, nursing homes. I bring fresh produce from the fruit and veg market in Overbridge to Ironash and distribute it." He waggled his finger at them, puffed up his chest. "And thanks to you, the old people will be hungry today."

"I'm sure they'll figure it out." Shona opened her notebook and tapped her pen on the first page that was covered in her small, neat handwriting. "Can you tell me what you were doing at the festival last night?"

"What everyone was doing. Listening to the bloody music."

"You always go? Each year?"

"Yeah, why?"

"I'm asking the questions, Mr Laghari."

He glared at her, unblinking.

He had an evil soul, Shona could see that in the depths of his eyes. He thought only of himself. He was as low as a man could get. So low, he could hardly be described as a man.

"At the festival," Shona went on, "you were seen tampering with a young woman's drink."

"What?" He stood, the chair legs scraping. "Who saw me? That's rubbish. They're lying."

"Sit down, Mr Laghari." Earle sat forward.

Samri's lips curled back, a weird snarl. He sat. "Whoever said that is making it the fuck up. Why the hell would I do that?"

"Do you have a girlfriend?" Shona asked.

"I can't see the relevance of that question." Samri tapped his fingers on the table, mimicking playing a super-fast tune on the piano.

"Please don't do that." Shona nodded at his fingers. "It will disturb the tape recording."

"I want to know who is accusing me of something I haven't done." He clasped his hands together. "And I want a solicitor."

Shona's phone rang. She answered it. "Hey, Darren."

"Thought you might want to know, ma'am, the witness and the victim of last night's suspected date rape have arrived. I've sat them in the family room."

"Great, thanks."

"And we have three officers and one member of admin with similar height, build, and complexion as the suspect. Would you like me to organise the lineup?"

"Yes, please." She looked at Samri. "The sooner the better." She ended the call.

"What's the sooner the better?"

"You confess, because when you're identified, you'll have no choice." She stood. "Interview terminated at ten-fifteen."

Earle also stood.

"So what am I supposed to do? Just sit here, behind these bars?" He nodded at the window which had iron strips covering the glass on the outside.

"Yes. But you should probably get used to that."

"I haven't fucking done anything wrong." He held out his hands. "Get that into your stupid head, woman."

She raised her eyebrows at him. "Do you want to find out what I'll do if you speak to me like that again?"

He folded his arms, and after glowering at Shona for a few seconds, turned away.

Thirty minutes later, Shona and Earle stood with Lina Davis and her friend, Sarah Cooper, who were staring through one-way glass.

On the other side, Samri Laghari glared straight ahead. To his right was a man of similar appearance but with a soft wave to his dark hair. And on Samri's left stood three other men, one a little too tall, one with a wedding ring Shona wished had been removed. At least dark jeans and a red t-shirt was uniform.

"Okay, ladies, the suspect is one of these men."

Lina shivered, and her friend put her arm around her.

"But don't worry, they can't see you," Shona said, resting her hand on Lina's shoulder. "All you need to do is identify the man who put the drug in the cola. Sarah, you saw him from an angle, is that right?"

Sarah nodded.

"We can get them to move left and right. If you want that, just say."

"I hardly saw him at all, really." Sarah nibbled on her bottom lip. "It's hard to remember."

Shona nodded and tamped down her frustration. "And Lina, try and think if one of these men was near you. Did the suspect speak to you, try and get close or learn about you before he slipped you the drug?"

She shook her head. Her cheeks were pale. "No, I've never seen any of them before."

Shona squeezed her hands into fists. The temptation to point Samri Laghari out to the witnesses was almost too much to bear.

"You said he was medium height with dark hair and you later remembered he was in these clothes or similar," Shona directed at Sarah.

"Yes." She kind of shrugged. "I think so. But it all happened so fast. And there were people in between us, it was a crowded place."

"But you saw what he did?" Shona asked.

"Yes, but that was his arm, his hand. After that it's a blur. I remember thinking I had to stop Lina drinking, but the first thing she did, before I could get to her, was gulp the drink back."

"It's all a fog." Lina hugged herself and leaned closer to Sarah. "Thank goodness for my friend. Goodness only knows what would have happened."

Things you wouldn't even want to imagine.

Shona turned to Earle.

He raised his shoulders a fraction and grimaced.

"Think hard. This is really important." Shona set her attention on the girls again. "We don't want him to be set loose, free to do this to others who won't be so lucky."

"No, no. I agree." Lina stared through the glass, her concentration intent. Then she sighed, and her body sagged. "No, I'm sorry. None of them ring a bell."

Shona resisted the urge to shout: *Not even the creepy arsehole of man second from the left?*

"Me neither." Sarah looked at Shona. "I'm really sorry. I just didn't get a good enough look, and not of his face."

Damn it.

"Okay," Shona managed through gritted teeth. "Thank you for your time, and Sarah, well done on your vigilance and taking care of Lina." She opened the door and sent the girls out into the care of a female uniform.

After she shut the door again, she plucked out her phone and dialled Darren. "No ID, suspect is free to go."

"Yes, ma'am."

She slipped her phone away and stomped to face the wall, her back to the lineup. "Fuck it!" She slapped the brickwork, the sting radiating over her palm and up to her shoulder. "Fuck it. Fuck it." She hit the wall again. Then gave it a kick for good measure, stubbing her left big toe so hard she knew it would bruise. That annoyed the hell out of her, so she kicked the wall again, with her right foot.

"Shona," Earle said, rushing to her side. "What the...?"

"Damn it. He's going to walk." She faced the window.

They were filing out. Samri stared at the one-way glass, a smug smile tilting his lips and his dark eyes flashing as if he were the Devil himself.

"That...bastard is getting away with it, and there's nothing we can do." She jabbed her finger towards the glass.

"Because we haven't got any evidence, nothing on him apart from being tall and dark with a red t-shirt and jeans."

"But I know he's guilty." She spun to Earle and rammed her hands on her hips.

"How?" He stared down at her. "How do you know?"

"I just do." She dragged both hands over her hair, her fingers catching in the long strands. "I just bloody do, okay?"

"No, not okay." He caught her elbows. "Tell me."

She clamped her lips together.

"Tell me." He was studying her face with such intensity.

"I can't." Her throat tightened, the defeat eating her alive.

"I'm here," he said, his voice softer. "Tell me how you know."

"Because..." She shook from his grip and took a step back. Her eyes misted. She hated that. She never cried, not over that night. What good did tears do?

"Because...?" Earle asked softly.

"Because he did it to me, okay, happy now?" she said. "That bastard dropped a roofie into my drink, eight years ago, right here in Ironash. He drugged me, took me somewhere, and did goodness knows what. And I know it's him. I just know..." Her words trailed off.

"Shit." Earle stared at her. "No wonder...at the festival..."

"I wanted to kill him. Yes. Wouldn't you have wanted to?"

He nodded. "Absolutely." He took a step closer, arms out.

"Don't even think about hugging me, it won't help."

He dropped his hands to his sides.

"What will help," she said, "is evidence on Samri Laghari and getting him off the streets. He's a danger to every female in Ironash. And I won't stop, I won't give in until I have him behind bars. I have to keep going...for them."

"Who? Who do you have to keep going for?"

"Nicola and Tina." Damn it, she'd said way too much. But she couldn't help it, the facts were spilling from her lips, she had to get them out. And if she was going to tell anyone, it might as well be her partner.

"Nicola and Tina are...?"

"My friends. The three of us were slipped something. He, Samri, and two of his friends took us away somewhere and...I have to catch him, for their sake."

"Him, don't you mean *them*?"

"I suppose so." She pursed her lips and blew out a breath. She needed to get a grip.

"So can't you see?" Earle said, gesturing to the empty lineup wall. "He was meant to walk today."

"How can that be?"

"He's walked so he can lead you to the others. Follow him, and we'll find the other two lowlifes. Why should any of them continue to roam Ironash?"

Shona stared at Earle. What he was saying made sense. If Samri Laghari was out on the streets they could keep an eye on him. See who he hung out with and where he went. His movements could be tracked, his whereabouts monitored.

"This was meant to happen," Earle said, his tone quiet and calm. "And from now on, you're not trying to figure this out on your own, Shona."

"I've always been trying to figure this out on my own. Nicola and Tina, they...haven't...it's complicated." She rubbed her stinging palms together. Her big toes hurt.

"Well, you're not on your own now. We'll find them and put them behind bars. I promise."

Shona managed a half smile. Earle couldn't make any such promises, but his determination came from the heart, and she knew she could count on him. He was a solid rock of a man. Someone she could trust. Someone who reminded her, despite the carnage she witnessed in her line of duty, that there were fine, upstanding people in the world who cared, who had morals, and would be at her side when she needed them most.

And going forward, she'd put money on needing Earle around, a lot.

"Thanks," she said quietly.

"For what?"

"Everything." She shrugged, managed a smile. "For being here, for being you."

ABOUT IRONASH

Ironash is a fictional town in the heart of England, now kept safer by the return of DI Shona Williams. And it's just as well, a lot of bad shit happens there!

#1 Sin, Repent, Repeat
#2 The Last Post
#3 Blind Panic

Follow A. J. Harlem on Amazon to get an alert when new books are released in the IRONASH series.

About the Author

A. J. Harlem is a bestselling author who has opened her vivid imagination to create thrilling British detective novels. She's always lived in the UK —England, Scotland and currently South Wales—and adores the colloquial use of the English language and quintessential settings for murder, crime and high drama. When she isn't writing her favourite past times generally revolve around her love of animals and include horse riding on the beach, walking her dogs in the Welsh mountains and flying birds of prey.

Printed in Poland
by Amazon Fulfillment
Poland Sp. z o.o., Wrocław